POLITICAL
Timber

OTHER BOOKS BY CHRIS LYNCH

CHRIS LYNCH

POLITICAL Timber

📖 HARPERCOLLINSPUBLISHERS

Library of Congress Cataloging-in-Publication Data
Lynch, Chris
 Political timber / Chris Lynch.
     p.   cm.
 Summary: High school senior Gordon Foley runs for mayor at the behest of his grand-
father, an old-style politician scheming to regain power while he's in prison for fraud.
 ISBN 0-06-027360-7. — ISBN 0-06-027361-5 (lib. bdg.)
 [1. Politics, Practical—Fiction.   2. Elections—Fiction.   3. Grandfathers—Fiction.]
I. Title.
PZ7.L979739Po   1996   96-5750
[Fic]—dc20   CIP
                                                                            AC
Typography by Al Cetta
1   2   3   4   5   6   7   8   9   10
❖
First Edition

CONTENTS

You could understand it if you ever drove the car. And if you ever got near my girlfriend, you'd understand it. Either experience would make it totally clear to you how I could ever have let it all happen to me. But you ain't never driven a Studebaker Gran Tourismo Hawk, and you ain't never—except maybe for a few of you— touched the cashmere small of Sweaty Betty's back, so I don't even know if you could ever quite know.

But here goes.

Tooling along up and over and down again and up again on the hills on the long road out of the town of Amber, a guy knows why it's so important to have a driver's license. The clouds follow the car, floating up higher when we crest a hill, coming back down on us when we valley out, lapping at the ice-white gleam of the Tourismo's hood like a big ol' tongue in the sky that just can't help itself but get a good lick in at the hood.

It is that kind of car. It's a delicious kind of a car.

And the road. You get the stomach wiggles every ten seconds from the perfect shwoop of the loll of the hills, curvalittle left, curvalittle right, rolling with it, swinging into it, but never *climbing*, because the grade never gets that steep, and the car never sweats. You could be driving over the skin of a giant bowl of chocolate pudding for all the resistance the road gives you.

The stereo plays, and it's a beautiful stereo, but it doesn't play loud, not on this road. That would insult the car, and it would be stupid. No, the music *accompanies* the auto.

Jeff Beck plays the guitar, just so. He's an old guy from long ago in the sixties, but he's got fine fingers like I'd kill for. He plays something called "Greensleeves," which is an old old tune from back in history somewhere, but which is a beautiful aural idea like I've never had myself.

The car, too, while we're at it, is from another time: 1963. Can you imagine?

One might suppose I was one of those lost-in-a-time-warp guys. Not true. I just take my pleasures, no questions asked, whence they come.

Which is a good point at which to get back to it. The point. Why I am on the luscious chocolate-pudding ribbon of road, in the white ice-cream car, listening to Mr. Beck pluck out "Greensleeves," is that I am on my way to visit the car's actual owner, who won't be needing it for the next five to fifteen years, and who always said that if anything ever happened to him, he wanted me to have the car.

"So," I'd said from my side of the Plexiglas when I'd last seen him. "So, I think this amounts to something *did* happen to you."

He'd laughed at me. Pulled the cigar out of his mouth—soaked and chewed and disintegrating as if a baby had been smoking it—and looked over his shoulder at the guard standing against the wall. "You believe this kid, Chuckie? My ass marks ain't even fluffed out of the driver's seat yet, and the kid's trying to take it away from me."

The guard laughed along, and shrugged. "Can't do nothing with kids, Fins. What're you gonna do?"

Fins turned back to me. "He's right. What am I gonna do?" He threw his hands straight up in the air, and laughed away as if somebody invisible was tickling his armpits.

That was what I loved about my grandfather. He could be in prison—even if it looked like a pretty luxurious prison—and have his own grandson trying to take his stuff, and still he thought it was funny. Even with the racketeering junk and all that, he was a belovable figure.

"I can have it then?"

"Ahhh, I don't know . . ." he teased. "That's a lot of car, a lot of responsibility. . . ."

"C'mon, Da. You know I'm the one. You know nobody's going to love it like I am. And Sweaty *adores* it."

He placed both hands flat on the partition. "Please, no talk of women, it's too frustrating for a guy in a place like this. You know there are no women allowed—no, y'know, conjugals. 'Cept Tuesdays, Thursdays, and weekends." He smiled his broad grin, with the large space between his front teeth.

"Da . . . ?" I whined.

"Ah," he said, shooing me away with both hands waving. "Go, take it. What am I, a convict, going to do about it? I have no power to stop you. No one is going to listen to me."

That was his joke. His no power. His nobody listening to him.

"Yo, Chuckie," he called to the guard. "Can I get a beer?"

The guard started out the door.

Fins turned to me. "I'm sorry. Gordie, you want one?"

Up until the day he went to jail, and for eighteen years prior to that, Fins Foley was the obscenely popular mayor of Amber. Had he known during all that time that there was a local ordinance against convicted felons holding municipal office, he would have fixed it in time to be the obscenely popular jailbird mayor of Amber.

"No, thanks, Da, I gotta be getting back. Sweaty's expecting me."

"Do *not* keep that young lady waiting," he said, fake-poking my little bony chest with his big bony finger.

"I won't," I said, kicking my aluminum chair over backward as I scrambled. "So," I treaded. "Can I tell her? That, y'know, the Hawk is mine."

". . . Till I get out, you mean? Can you take care of it for me, you mean?"

"I mean that, yes," I said.

4

"Don't I give you everything? Am I not a complete sucker when it comes to my favorite relative?"

Truth? He is. Total sucker. For me alone.

"No way. You're tough as nails."

"Get outta my prison," he said, shaking a fist and biting his sopping cigar in half. "Ya rotten punk."

Just as the door was about to close behind me, and Fins was telling the guard how wicked his grandson was, just as I was about to pull a Batman leap from the second-story window right into the seat of—

Did I mention the Gran Tourismo Hawk was a convertible?

"Hey, hey, hey," he called.

Slowly I pushed the door open just enough to slip my narrow head and shoulders through.

"If I hear tires spinning in that parking lot, I will escape. I will break a wall, and run, and even with Chuckie here on my back, I will catch up to you on foot."

"I would *want* you to beat me up, Da."

"A car—the right car—can be the most important thing in a young man's life."

"Next to his grandpa," I slobbered. Shameless.

"Don't get jerky on me now."

"I'll never forget . . ." I said, backing out.

He didn't even have to yell for me this time. He held up one finger, as if he had been struck by an idea.

"How old are you now, Gordie?"

"Seventeen."

"When are you eighteen?"

I came all the way back down to earth as I heard the seldom-oiled gears of my grandfather's mayoral-racketeer thought machine.

"This is gonna cost me, isn't it?"

"Whaaat, whaaat?" He sounded hurt. Sipped his beer. "Stop already. When are you eighteen?"

"Next week. Da, you *know* that. You've never ever missed my birthday. You know it better than my parents do."

He chuckled. He loved being compared to my parents. It only made him look even more immense.

"You come in and see me on your birthday. Will you do that for a poor tired old man? A sad, unjustly accused—"

"I'll come, I'll come," I said. "*Now* can I go see my girlfriend?"

He nodded.

"I love you," he said.

"Shit. I love you, Da," I said, through the protection of the steel door.

"I love you," he said again, because he always has the last word. And because it was true. Which was why whatever he had planned for me was inevitable. I could never tell him no.

"Come on, Betty."

"Come on yourself. What's your problem today?" She pushed me away firmly with both hands, pinning me to the driver-side door. Sweaty Betty was at least as strong as me.

I struggled toward her again, but could not get myself out of the hold. I relented, hung there like a poster tacked to the wall.

"Please?" I wailed.

"It's the middle of the day, Gordie. What are you thinking? All of a sudden it's like you got some irresistible charisma or something? I think I can resist it."

The window was rolled halfway down, enough for me to poke my head out and look up at the meltaway clouds while my body remained stuck. We—Sweaty Betty, the Studebaker, and myself—were parked at a quiet, breezy spot a quarter mile from the school, peaceful, but not really private enough for me to be asking for what I was asking for at three in the afternoon.

"Hey, Gordie, sorry, man," Mosi said, looking down into my face, blocking out the entire sky with his massive, frizz-framed head. "Just heard, about Fins losing the appeal. Everybody knows he didn't do it."

"Thanks, Mos." I maneuvered my arm up through the window beside my head, and engaged Mosi in a firm wrist-shake. "But what if he *did* do it?"

He shrugged, as if this were irrelevant. "Screw 'em then, if they can't take a joke."

Mosi leaned out over the windshield before he left. "Hi, Sweaty," he said, and lumbered away.

"Hey, Mosi," she answered, finally releasing me.

"He said I could keep it," I said, toggling my head around to loosen my neck. "The Tourismo. Fins says it's mine."

"Get *out*," she returned.

"True it is, baby baby." As Sweaty Betty's face lit up, I inflated and grew suave and slick, taking on the personality of the Gran Tourismo Hawk. She turned away from me now, giving all her attention to the car. Lightly, with the tips of three fingers, she caressed the walnut, red leather, and polished—polished by *me*, twice a week—chrome of the dashboard. Back and forth and back and forth, her long slim hand stroked the surface, running along from the glove compartment that was big enough to carry a sleeping bag, to the radio with the tubes inside that took three minutes to warm up before it would play anything. She stopped there, diddled the metallic station buttons like piano keys, then snapped back around to me.

"He did not, you lying sack," she said.

"Huh? Huh? . . . Unnn-huh?"

I had frozen, fixed and dilated, on her fingers and what they had done for the Hawk. I almost didn't need her anymore.

"Fins didn't give you the Stude. No way."

"He did, I swear. But I think it's gonna cost me something. I'm not sure what, but I have to go see him on my birthday."

She looked at me differently now, piercingly. Very exciting, very frightening. "So it's really true, then. You and the Tourismo. You are one. You don't just borrow it now."

I nodded. My new charisma smile.

"Hey, sorry to hear about Fins, man." The voice came in the window from over my shoulder. I didn't even know who it was.

"Get outta here, you," Sweaty snapped at him, without taking her eyes off me.

"*Happy* birthday, young man," Fins hollered as I stepped into the visitors' room.

"Ya, happy birthday, kid," the guard said.

"Thanks, Da," I said, bouncing on the balls of my feet, shooting the old guy with my finger gun. Then I trained it on the guard. "And, thanks, ah . . . Chuckie." Bang. Shot him. Holstered the pistol and sat in my chair backward.

"Eighteen," Fins said, nodding. "Sonofabitch."

"Eighteen." I nodded.

"You're a man now."

"Was a man before."

"But a real, official one now."

"All that and more, Finian."

I was eighteen, I was driving the Hawk. I was taking the day off from school. It was a cloudless October day as summery as anything June could do. Life was so good, I could feel its fingers running up my frontals and down my back.

"You're beaming, kid. You got a glow."

"Do I?" I checked my look as well as I could in the scratched Plexiglas. "I know I can feel it, but does it show, really?"

"Chuckie, does the man got a glow?" Fins called back over his shoulder.

"I can't hardly stand it. He's hurtin' my eyes."

"See that, stop it now, Gordie, your hurting the officer's eyes. He's gonna put on the shades any second, and there ain't nothing more depressing than one of them big cop types following you around all day wearing the mirror shades indoors."

"Slinging with both hands today, Da," I said, closing one eye like I was about to get hit. "What're you going to drop on me?"

"Relax. Will you relax? I got a present for you, on account of you're eighteen now and a legally recognized man."

I smiled in anticipation. My grandfather was a creative and flamboyant gift-giver, even when he didn't build up the moment like this.

"Chuckie, could you please?" he asked the guard as he drew an envelope out of his pocket. The guard came and took it, let himself out the special no-entry door that separated Fins Foley from Gordie Foley, and slipped me the paper. Quickly he got back to the incarceration side of the wall, since he really wasn't supposed to allow Fins to give me stuff. But it was my big one-eight.

I read the form that was inside the envelope. It made no sense to me.

"This makes no sense to me, Da."

"Read it again," he said. "It's kind of important that you can read, and comprehend stuff."

"Nomination form?"

"That's right."

" 'Gordon Foley.' That's me, my name there at the top."

"Correct."

"Who am I nominating?"

"Gordon Foley."

"Gordon Foley," I echoed.

"Gordon Foley." That echo would not go away.

I stared at the form, trying harder and harder to comprehend, but the more intensely I stared at the words, the more intensely they resisted me. I looked up from them to Fins, who now had one cigar clenched in his teeth and one pointed at me.

Chuckie the guard—whose name tag read V. McGonnigal—came around again and stuck the kielbasa cigar in my gaping orifice.

"I got a couple parking tickets—think you could fix 'em for me?" he joked. I think.

"Happy birthday, kid." Fins beamed like a new father. "You're gonna be goddamn mayor."

"So what did he give you?"

Sweaty had been waiting in the car while I visited my grandfather. When I returned, she had the top down and the front passenger seat reclined all the way back to where it was lying on top of the rear seat. Her feet were crossed up on the dashboard.

"Didn't I tell you no feet on the dashboard, Betty," I snapped, pulling her feet down. I pulled the chamois cloth out of the glove compartment and started buffing.

"Come on, come on, what did you get? A big wad of money? A house? What?"

I couldn't concentrate until I had finished polishing up the dash. There.

"Um." I tried to assemble it in my own mind, then to frame it for Sweaty. "The city. He, pretty much, gave me the city."

"I wasn't aware he owned it. Damn generous of him."

"Ya, well, eighteen is one of the big ones. And he does like me a lot."

"Great," she said, hopping up straight in her seat

and pumping it back to upright position. "Let's go play with your new present."

Already Betty was enjoying the whole thing more than I was. This wasn't good. I wanted to get it too. This was where I should have been fired up, peeling out of the lot with Sweaty on my lap, making for the beach. But . . .

"Wait here," I said, trotting in reverse from the car back toward the prison.

Sweaty Betty took her sunglasses off once more and maneuvered the seat back into sunbathing position. I saw her wave way up high past me. I turned to see three or four somebodies waving back from behind a fence on the roof of the building.

"Better hurry," she called.

" 'Cause, as you know, Gordie, they aren't letting me be mayor anymore, even though everybody wants me to be."

"I heard," I said, staring again at my name on the form. "So why do I fall into it?"

" 'Cause you're what I need. You remind me a lot of me a long time ago. You're young, you're cute, you'll be a statement. And I've learned, when it's really important, you can only trust family."

"So, Da, why not run my dad? *He's* your son."

"Him? I wouldn't trust him as far as I could throw him."

So much for the family thing.

"See, I had what they call in the papers a 'hand-picked successor,' but,"—he let out a dramatic, wounded sigh—"she ain't turning out too great. She's kind of ignoring the boss now she thinks I'm outta the way."

I waved my hands at him, crosswise, like *stop, stop!* "That's all fine, Da. But frankly it's not the part I'm interested in. What I want to know *right now*"—I pointed both index fingers at the floor beneath me, at the here and now, in case he missed my point—"is what are you doing to *me*? What is going to happen to me here? I'm a senior now, you know. I kind of had plans for this year."

"What do you think? Think I don't know? Think the old Da's so decrepit I don't remember? I know what your plans are. One big party, puffing your chest out and pulling your pants down, now till May, am I right?"

"Ohhh." I was about to get indignant when the words registered. "Well, ya. I mean, you make it sound kind of stupid, but I suppose that's about it."

He beamed. "See. I been there. And know what? My plan is just going to help you. Jesus, Gordie, you know what it's going to be like, going through senior year as an eighteen-year-old political superstar? You'll be beating 'em off with a stick."

Superstar.

I let him do it to me. The old snake.

"You'll be goddamn near godlike. Hell, I only *wish* I could have been mayor at eighteen instead of—"

"Whoa. Stop right there for a second. Eighteen-year-old mayor. Da, you're talking like I'm going to *win*. That's not going to happen, is it? You're not going to make me win, are you?"

Fins stood up, stretched his arms high and wide, groaned like a waking bear.

"Don't sweat so much. It's not becoming to a candidate for public office to perspire. You don't have to win, anyhow. You're going to run a very strong race. Early polls are going to show you opening up a respectable lead, throwing a mighty scare into your opponent. You will become the season's phenomenon. Newspaper's going to call you a juggernaut, but don't be offended, 'cause it's better than it sounds. Then, Sheena of the political jungle, my former protégée, will come in here and pay me a visit during which she will say the right things. Following that reconciliation, your candidacy will waver, then falter—or maybe it's falter, then waver. Anyway, in the end you will go down to a very narrow, yet very noble, defeat."

I thought about it, rode the whole ride on his words. I could see the thing play out, kind of a fun ride, with no resulting responsibility. A potential hoot.

And coincidentally, a hoot was precisely what I had in mind for the year.

"Cool," I said. "Think there's any way I could fina-gle some kind of school credit out of it?"

Fins grinned, turned to Chuckie the guard, then back to me.

"Kid, you're going to be great at this."

T ruth was, I was always considered to be a very responsible guy by the small core of people who got close to me. But since most of them were musicians or people with no discernible hobby, avocation, or place to go, being responsible meant I was the one who wore a watch.

"Mayor?" Mosi screamed over his own distorting amp, at the back of his mattress-padded garage. "I didn't even know the school had a mayor. That's the balls."

I strummed, much more quietly, on an acoustic guitar from Mosi's collection of instruments, which stood upright on guitar stands all around us like rock-'n'-roll Stonehenge. I really couldn't play much; mostly hung around with people who could.

"They don't, Mos. I'm talking about, of the city. Amber. Mayor of Amber."

"Get outta town."

"I can't. I'm gonna run it."

Mosi nodded his great shaggy head, squinting hard as the smoke from the cigarette rolled back over his face. "Can I be police chief?" he asked, studying his fingers on the fretboard.

"Sorry," I said. "Promised Sweaty."

"School superintendent?"

"Hmmm. It's yours."

"Excellent. I'm gonna do some big-ass firing first day."

Flexible Campus is basically the plum of all senior-year plums, where you get to take two days a week out of school to apply to a more worldly, adult pursuit. But you have to present them with a decent plan, like apprentice in an architectural firm, volunteer at a hospital, teach a gym class at a blind school, stuff like that. A lot of kids with no imagination take college classes to get a jump on next year. Yawn. Myself, I was going to try to get into a radio station, maybe learn to work an audio board, wear big professional head-phones, get the jock to make jokes about me on air so I could be famous. It was the best-thought-out plan in the program.

But that was before.

I took my seat in Mr. Vadala's office. Vadala was coordinator of the Flexible Campus program, and the career-track guidance counselor, the one who didn't want to hear about why you'd been passing out cold in homeroom but would give you a thirty-page printout on the best vocational training programs in the country. In his way, he was the most practical, functional, useful guy on the faculty. Zero shit content, ol' Vadala.

He looked like a retired catcher, broad and squat with fat clumps of curly hair springing up over the collar of his shirt and around the back of his neck. Thinner clumps on the top of his head, which you stared into as he pored over his computer files.

"Mr. Vadala? Ah, I'm here."

"I know you are. Be with you in a second." Unlike most people, Vadala kept his computer directly in front of him, like a castle wall, so you had to conduct your business with him over it.

He looked up at me. Removed his glasses and rubbed the two residual red marks on the sides of his shark-fin nose.

"Foley," I said, helping him along. "Gordon Foley."

"Foley," he answered, hit four keys. "Have I seen you before, Foley?"

"Hope so," I said. "Been here four years."

"Hmmm." Vadala leaned in close to the green screen. "I'm sorry, Mr. Foley, but I have no recollection of seeing you before."

"Don't sweat it," I said. "That's sort of the kind of profile I was after."

"Here you are." He pointed at the computer screen. "Foley, Gordon. But there's nothing here, I'm afraid, Gordon. I keep fairly complete records of the student body, and, well . . . anyway, what can I do for you? You're here to pitch your Flex-Campus plan, I imagine."

"I am."

"Shoot."

"I'm going to be mayor."

Mr. Vadala's hirsute fingers were already working the keyboard, finally plugging me in there with the rest of the fully functioning student body, when he stopped. "Gordon, this is a very busy time for me, with all your classmates making presentations the same week. Now, I like a good joke as much as the next guy—just a half hour ago one guy proposed that he'd be spending Tuesdays and Thursdays working in quality control at the Sam Adams brewery. I laughed. Another said he was going to spend the two days a week in a sleep-study over at the Deaconess hospital. A young lady told me that if I would allow her to expand her Flex-Campus from two days to three, she would spend the extra day with me at my house."

That tears it: She does *not* get the police chief job.

"But I'm serious, Mr. Vadala."

"You're serious. You mean to tell me you're going to spend your senior year—" He stopped himself, staring at me. Put his glasses back on. "Whoa, wait a minute." Back to the keyboard. He flew so authoritatively over the keys, it sounded like a tiny little Thoroughbred race. "Ah. The annex file tells the story. You're *that* Foley."

I sighed. I could see the political-legacy thing was going to be a burden, bringing knowing leers from everybody.

"So then," Vadala chuckled, now keying in my

proposal. "You're not only going to run, then, you're going to *win*."

"No way, I'm—" I stopped myself when he turned a concerned look my way. "Of course I'm going to win. You don't enter a race like this if you don't expect to win it, dammit." To bone up on attitude, I'd stayed up to watch *The Last Hurrah* the night before.

"Okay, Foley, Tuesdays and Thursdays you're a full-time candidate. But remember, the other days you're still a student."

"No I'm not. I'm a senior."

Vadala opened his mouth to snap at me, then let it soften into a gentle, ugly smile.

"Okay, that was a good one."

I shook his hand when he stood.

"And at the end, you still owe me a report, just like everybody else. At least try to learn a small something from your experience."

I continued to pump his hand. Practicing. And ignored what he was saying while I concentrated on making my pitch. Still practicing.

"So I hope I can count on your vote come election day," I campaigned, through my wide, cheesy smile.

He sat down, spoke into his computer.

"Well . . . it's not important to your grade, anyway."

I passed Mosi on my way out. I gave him the thumbs-up, which caused him to charge right in.

"I'm going to be working in the incoming mayor's administration," I heard him say.

"I do not care to listen to another joke proposal," Vadala popped.

"Hey, you. You don't want to piss me off," Mosi barked. "*You* just might come begging into *my* office after the election."

He sounded awfully close to believing all this.

"No direction, huh?" I said to my dad as he came through the front door. I had his big easy armchair dragged over to the front door, where I sat regally, mayorally, awaiting him. "Just getting by? No master plan? No ambition?"

"You joined the debate team," he said hopefully.

I shook my head. "Debate's so *negative*."

The phone rang.

"Let the machine get it," I said.

He could never let the machine get it.

"Try it, one time, Dad," I said as he hurdled me and the chair to get to it. "I don't remember us ever getting one single phone call that couldn't have waited. Not—"

He held up his index finger to me, squinting a smile and nodding a nonverbal *Just a sec*.

"Yes, he's here," he said, aiming the phone at me.

"Fine," I said, shoving the chair all the way back across the room and taking my sweet time about it like the potential city employee I was. He'd spoiled my moment.

"Ya," I said, bratty.

"Gordon Foley?"

"Gordon Foley."

"Hello, Gordon, this is Matt Baker, at station WRRR."

"Wrrr!" I growled automatically, the response you're supposed to give to win free CDs and concert tickets and stuff.

"Nah, Gordon, it's not that. I'm calling because you applied for an internship here at the station. This is you, right?"

Jesus, I thought, the old plan. Does it figure, or what? Soon as you light up, the damn bus comes along.

"Ya. Gordon Foley, right. This is me. Gordon Foley."

My first attempt at filling dead airtime. Good thing I wasn't applying as a jock.

"Good, kid. We've established you're Gordon Foley. The question is, are you still interested?"

"Am I still interested?"

I held out my two hands flat and spread wide, weighing one against the other. Mayor, radio? Mayor, *radio*? Mayor, radio, mayor, radio, mayor, rock RADIO?

"What are you *doing*?" my father asked, staring at me and mimicking my motions.

I held up a finger to him. *Just a sec, Dad.*

"Shit ya, I'm still interested."

"Of course you are. You're a kid, right? You're an American, right?"

"Is that required?" I asked.

"Ha, you're funny, too. I got one more question for you. You listed one 'Fins Foley' as a reference—"

"Yes, he's *that* Fins Foley."

"Relation?"

"Sí, señor."

"Okay, well, you know, we might want to talk about him some on the show. Might even be a little . . . irreverent. 'Zat gonna be a problem for you?"

Irreverent? To my da? Not only was that unheard of around Amber—at least while Fins was a free-walking citizen—it was scary. Matt Baker was "irreverent" on his show a lot, and made cops and hockey players and other ruffian guests cry right there on the air.

My da? My mentor?

Girls, radio, rock and roll, girls, senior year, rock and roll, girls, radio.

"Not a problem, Matt."

What *was* a problem, only I hadn't thought about it until after hanging up, was how was I going to go to school, work two days at the station, and, oh ya, run for mayor?

was at school.

I was in the Hawk.

I was on the phone.

He made me take it, the little black folding flippy thing that was about as big as three credit cards taped together end-to-end-to-end. I might as well not even run if I didn't have one, he said, because nobody who matters doesn't have a cellular phone. And when I didn't have a call, I was to pretend. I didn't have to pretend often, though, since he called me constantly.

"So you got your nosebones, who have always voted for us and always will. You listening to me, Gordie? Okay, you got your nosebones, your sweet boys, and your delicious chickens—"

"Da?"

I cupped my hand over the mouthpiece, as if that was the way to keep anyone from overhearing him.

"What, Gordie? What's the problem?"

"Those . . ." I leaned closer to the dashboard. "Those *things* you're saying."

"Well, it's true. Learn who you are in the political universe, Gordie. You are a Foley. Therefore you are a liberal, a populist. So your core constituency is going to be the nosebones and swishies and delicious chickens and Cambos and all the other marginalized fringies. And, of course, the bleeding hearts that come suckling along behind 'em."

"Jesus, Da. How can you—"

"What? I said something wrong?"

I knew better than this. I was not going to slice open this seventy-year-old can of worms. I heard my father once try to discuss the "label" issue with him. He labeled my father in ways a kid should not have to hear.

"Okay, Da, as long as we don't have to have this discussion again. I have a question, though. Delicious chickens?"

"Ya, delicious chickens. Chicks. Dames. Like, the League of Delicious Chicken voters, who, by the way, will be endorsing you—in a stunning coup—over my opponent. Who, you may have noticed, is herself a delicious chicken."

"My opponent."

"Huh?"

"My opponent. You said *your* opponent, but you're not running."

"Oh, I did not. Of course you're running. Your opponent."

"Right, well, back to my constituency."

"The common man," Da crowed proudly. "The disenfranchised. The little guy. The guy who feels like the government ignores him at the expense of every-body else."

I liked the sound of it. I listened to him rhapsodize on the American sense of fair play and equality as I kicked back in the Studebaker, aimed into the bright morning sun, and watched my passing classmates as they watched me. Every eye in the parking lot snapped my way as I plotted political history on my very cool little bitty phone. As I watched them all, and listened to him, I was momentarily dazzled, as if the sun had just shattered the Gran Tourismo Hawk's thirty-year-old windshield into a million suspended crystals.

Suddenly I understood. The thing the Kennedys have always understood: I could do truly good works for the betterment of all peoples; and I could get all the delicious chickens in the process.

My grandfather was laughing heartily. I saw the guys and gals outside my window smiling too, and realized that I was laughing along with Fins.

"And the beauty of it for you and me is"—he could barely choke out the words—"that that includes everybody. You tell 'em you're running to stick up for the little guy, the disenfranchised, and every jamoke on the street thinks that's him."

My grandfather was still laughing at the great ironic high he got out of politics, when a girl I didn't know pulled open my car door. I recognized her as a cheerleader—I'd torn the page out of the library's copy of the yearbook—and a junior. The two girls with her looked to be likewise underclasspersons.

"This your car?" she asked, without looking at me. She was looking all around the car's interior, like she was thinking of buying.

I stared at her cherubic, freckled, satanic cheer-leader face. I pressed the phone hard to my ear the way I clutch the arms of the dentist's chair trying to reroute unwanted sensations.

"Gotta go, Da," I said stiffly. He just went on and on, telling me something about . . . something campaign related.

"Is this an electric top?" She played one ungodly long white-polished fingernail underneath the toggle switch that moved the roof. "How come I never seen you here before, huh? You ain't a freshman, are you?"

"Don't touch that," I said.

It didn't matter how many cartwheels she could do. This was the Tourismo, for god's sake.

I reached out to block her hand from contacting any of the car's controls, and immediately the three of them started laughing at me.

The flip phone had stuck to my ear, held by the nervous suction pressure I'd created.

Two of the girls walked away immediately. The third lingered.

"Nice ride," she hummed, before following her friends. "Call me, when the phone is free again."

"Da, I have to go," I snapped, popping the phone off my head. "Gotta go work the underclasses."

"There, that's the populist spirit," he was saying when I folded him up and rolled him in my T-shirt sleeve.

"Betty, Christ, I was just trying to get their votes." I ducked as I spoke, and shielded my head with my arms. Sweaty Betty is a slapper.

"How-are-you-sup-posed-to"—one slap per syllable—"win-votes-from-fif-teen-year-old-hood-sies-who-can't-vote?"

Candidate caught with hand in cookie jar.

We were in the stands high above football practice. A couple dozen head of overfed underloved stud cattle looked up from whacking each other to watch the better action in the bleachers. Mosi, from out of the clouds, swooped in between us before Betty had the chance to sneak in that potent little uppercut of hers. Boos came from the field.

"Because," Mosi drawled, thinking on the fly, "because he wasn't working on his mayor gig, he was working on his student-body-president gig."

See that? Most people think Mosi's a little slow. *I* know he's a genius.

Sweaty turned to me. I turned to Mosi. Mosi turned up to the sky.

"Since when?" she demanded of me.

"I just figured, it made sense. If I was gonna—"

"That's a 'why' answer, Gordie. We're not up to that yet. I asked you a 'when' question."

"I just nominated him today," Mosi chirped.

"That's enough out of you, mouthpiece."

"He just nominated me today," I said. Then I remembered the real campaign. "Nomination papers. *Shit*," I said.

"What's your problem?" Betty asked.

"I forgot I was supposed to go see my grandfather after school today. He has my nomination papers with the three hundred signatures I needed."

Mosi laughed out loud. "You had Fins get your signatures for you? From *jail*?"

I shrugged. "He said it was no trouble. He doesn't have a shitload to do at the moment. Anyhow"—I looked at my watch—"between school and the radio station and my campaign—*both* campaigns—I just can't do it all."

I started down the bleachers, walking over the aluminum benches. "In fact, I have to fly right now. I'll have to go right to WRRR from the jail. Today's my orientation."

Mosi followed me.

"So, that nomination thing is all in order, then, Mos?"

"Ah, ya," he said. "I'll just pop back in and make sure it all got done in time." He took off across the field toward the main building. The quarterback sailed a ball at Mosi, a fat wobbler that missed his head by three feet as he galloped off. Our quarterbacks always sucked.

Betty stepped up close behind me as we neared the bottom of the steep bank of stands. Just then the cheerleaders filed onto the field, across our line of vision, right to left.

I did not turn my head to look at them. I felt the strain on my neck muscles as my brain, like a big dog on a leash, tried to yank my head in that direction. But I was strong, trembling with the tension.

Sweaty clomped me across the back of the head anyway.

"Cool. So this is it, right? Just file this downtown, then I can sit back and ride out the election?"

Fins furrowed his big meaty brow and shook his head at me. "Gordie, boy, there is work involved here. This is going to be quite a ride for the next couple of months. The runoff goes down in a month, and the special election one month after that. You'll have help, sure, but you gotta at least be *visible* the whole time."

I rubbed my forehead, which was starting to ache every day now about twenty minutes after I awoke. "Visible. Da, what's visible? You got three hundred people to sign for me here in, what, two days? How hard could this be? Just go on and tell the rest of your fans to vote for me on election day and we're all set, right?"

The brow again, and the head shaking.

"So make a few extra phone calls. No offense, but—you got the time."

"Gordie, you know how many people are in this town? I mean, you're looking to run the city, I suppose you should know how big it is. Huh, how many, you think?"

"Jeez. I dunno, Da. A lot."

"How big a lot?"

"A whole lot. A wicked lot."

"Gordon?"

When he calls me *Gordon* . . .

"All right . . . twelve thousand people."

"Excellent guess, Mr. Mayor. There are seventy-eight thousand people in this city."

"Holy shit," I said. I hopped up out of my chair, as if to escape the throng.

My grandfather was amused. "Hey, how 'bout this one," he said, leering. "Guess what the city budget is for this year?"

"I gotta go to the bathroom, Da."

"One hundred million dollars," he crowed. "Want to know how many schools we have?"

"*No, I don't.* They got bathrooms here, Da, or is that part of the punishment? . . ."

"Police? Parks-department no-show grounds-keepers?"

I stopped thinking about the toilet, threw myself against the Plexiglas partition. "Da, what are you doing to me? I just wanted something interesting to do on Tuesdays and Thursdays. I just wanted girls to like me."

"Easy, bubby," my dear old grandfather said. "Your da is going to be with you all the way. So stop fretting. We can't have you getting worry lines already. Your skin is your strongest political asset." He leaned closer to me, where my face was still mushed to the partition. "You have great skin. Easy on the fried clams, though. I see a blind zit bubbling up on ya."

I backed up, felt around for the zit. Started worrying more.

"Next meeting, we'll strategize. I got your itinerary laid out nice. But now you go home and sleep. That's your job, and you're gonna need it."

I agreed, even though that was impossible. My job was not sleeping, it was working at the station.

Wrrr.

My guy, Matt, was the night guy. Which meant I was going to have to be a night guy too. Seven to midnight twice a week. Tuesdays and Thursdays, theoretically, but since my calendar was starting to get pretty jammed, Matt said we could flex it however I needed to. I thought that was awfully decent of him.

My actual instructor, the guy who sat next to me at the controls and showed me what to do, was a guy named Sol. He was a very serious, technician-type guy who didn't seem to appreciate that he was in show business and that it was a privilege to have the city's most controversial deejay making fun of his relatives and stuff over the air. Sol was very skinny all over except for his belly, which poked out from under a T-shirt that never quite managed to reach all the way down to his belt-line. His stomach was very hairy, like a sweater, and he never smiled. Like a jazz musician or a boxer, Sol could have been thirty-five or sixty-five, you couldn't tell. What was very clear was that his attitude had already reached retirement age.

Sol didn't like me at first.

"See that cable there. If you touch it, you'll get electrocuted. Touch it if you want."

Sol, I was to learn, felt that every curious kid who walked in the door was after his job.

"Hey, Sol," Matt yelled when I first walked in. "Pack it in, old boy, your replacement's here." Which didn't help.

"You think it's all fun, right?" Sol asked as we were setting up for my first night of actual live-on-the-air work after two dry runs. "You kids, you think the audio techs just kick back, push buttons, drink coffee, and listen to the jock make an ass out of himself. Then we collect a fat check, cash it at the White Hen across the street, and take the dough around the corner to the bar, where we tell all the girls we're a hot-shit radio professional."

On the rare occasions you run into a guy as blunt as Sol, it is hard not to give him the same in return.

"That's exactly what I think. Except I didn't even know the White Hen would cash my check. That's cooler still."

The first I'd seen of Sol's sinister smile curled over one corner of his square mouth. I heard a low rumbly laugh as he went on with his preshow prep. Then he pulled a microphone and stand out of a green plastic trash barrel full of knotted wires and gadgets. He set up the mike right in front of me.

"What's the deal here?" I asked as I began playing with the equipment. "Test," I barked. "Hi, Mom."

Sol just continued that unsettling little chuckle.

"No, really, Sol. Why do I have a microphone? I didn't have one during dry run."

On the other side of the glass wall that separated the technicians from the on-air talent, Matt strode into the room and took his seat at the desk.

Matt turned toward me, gave me two thumbs-up.

I waved, then pointed to the microphone in front of me, mouthing, *What is this?*

He thumbed me up a little farther, ignored my question, and flashed an incandescent smile.

I noted that he had spectacular teeth for a guy who was on radio instead of TV.

"Goooood evening, boys and girls!" Mad Matt yelled into his microphone. It pierced my eardrums. Sol handed me a stick of gum.

"Have I got a treat for you, loyal fans. Right here in our studio, and for an extended engagement, we have got THE NEXT MAYOR OF AMBER!"

Matt swung around to leer at me, eyeballs as white as his teeth.

"Jesus Christ," I yelped, and I heard it in my headset. I was on the air.

"There you go, Amber, another politician with a messiah complex. Boy's a natural for the job."

I held my head in my hands, staring straight ahead at Mad Matt. Beside me, Sol's laugh picked up a little speed and volume. Sounded like a twenty-year-old Chevette idling at a stoplight.

Matt waved at me to speak. When I didn't—couldn't—he helped me out.

"Word has it the kid's a juggernaut. First he's going to sweep the high school president's race, then stop by and pick up the conveniently available mayor's job. Can the White House really be far off? And why shouldn't he have it in his blood? Do we know who this boy's grandpappy is? I'll tell you who he is, he's . . . whoa, whoa, slow down there, Mad Matt. You haven't even let the boy introduce himself. Tell us, scion, what is your name?"

"Gordie," I chirped.

"Is that sweet, or what? Amber, meet Mayor Gordie. Huh? Won't work, ya say? Okay. Yo, Gordie, think you could let us in on the rest of it?"

To the world, or to the part of it that was listening, I'm certain that it sounded as if Mad Matt was interviewing a mental defective just to get laughs—which would not be out of line with what he normally does on his show. But to me, inside my headphones, which were acting like corks to trap all the desperate thoughts in my skull, it was more like this:

Jesus, Jesus, Jesus. What? Shit? Huh? Howdidithappen, howdidithappen, howdidithappen? He knew. Sonofabitch. Set me up. Sonofabitch. What works best? If I shut up I look stupid. If I run . . . no. What if I cry? That diddler cop who cried on the show got a lot of sympathy afterward. . . .

"Just a name, Gordie? I mean, is it one of those obscene-sounding names with no vowels in it?"

"F-F-Foley." I spat all over my microphone.

"*There* you go, boys and girls. Gordie Foley. Now, should I tell you who his granddad is? Nope. Lines are open, you all tell me."

Matt punched a button, Sol pushed a couple of levers, and music filled the air.

I keeled over onto the console.

Sol pulled me back up by my shirt collar so I could see the boss grinning at me, winking, and circling his fingers into the okeydokey sign, as if we were all in on this terrific cool joke. Except, of course, that I wasn't in on it. I *was* it.

"*Hello*, you're on the air."

"Ya, hi. I know who he is. Is his grandfather *@#%-face Foley?"

The station operated on a seven-second delay. Being an insider now, I was privileged to here the pre-beep filth.

"Yes, you are absolutely right, Gordie's granddad is none other than famous felon *@#%-face Foley himself."

"Hey, Matt. Come on . . ." I finally spoke up. More or less.

"No, no, no, Gordie, we're just having a little fun here. I love old Fins. Everybody does. I even voted for him. I had to; his goons came to my house."

"Well," I said, by way of defending the Foley family honor, "I don't know about that. But *I* don't have any goons, I can assure you."

"Oh, that's sad. Hell, buck up, kid, maybe you'll get some goons of your own for your birthday."

"My birthday's already passed."

Great, Gord. Sharp. I was for sure going to have to work on this repartee business if I was going to last in either of my new endeavors. Sol was openly laughing at me now. Oddly this cheered me, seeing him loosen up finally.

"On second thought, why wait? My listeners have always been generous to needies in the past. Let's get on the phones, kids. Crack open those piggy banks. The drive starts here. Get Gordie some goons—call in your pledges and suggestions now."

He threw on some music, rolled his chair back from his desk, and made his way toward me. I was dripping with sweat, exhausted, slumped in my chair, my nose resting on my knee. It was seven fifteen.

Matt sat up on the edge of the control deck in front of me. He slapped my shoulder.

I made a move to slap him back. Caught myself.

"So, Gordie, you want to quit?"

"*@#% yes!" I yelled.

"Don't."

"Ya? That's it, 'Don't'? Pretty persuasive there, Mr. Matt."

"What did you come here for?"

"I'm a senior. I want girls to want me, and I want guys to be jealous of me."

Matt nodded, stared off wistfully. "I hear you. I

wouldn't trade my senior experience for anything. Those two years were hotter than all the rest combined."

"Ya. Well, song's running down, Matt. You better get back out there and start zooing me and my family again."

"Gordie, you knew the kind of show I do. You *wanted* to be a part of it." He leaned in closer now, put his small smooth hand on my shoulder. "And you were right to want to. Tell me, what's in your future? You gonna be . . . *ma-yor?*" Matt laughed, Sol laughed, I laughed. "Or would you maybe like to get in The Show somewhere?"

I didn't have to answer. He knew. I knew. I don't know if Sol knew, but it didn't matter since he didn't give a *@#%.

Matt was all too aware of what goes on inside little skinny guys who can't play guitar but more than anything want to play guitar. We just want to be *in the vicinity.* That much Mad Matt and I shared.

"Good, stay," he said, straightening up. "You aren't going to regret it. And I'll let you in on something—"

Finally, I thought, he's letting me in on something.

"There ain't no such thing as bad fame. The point of getting on my show? Is getting on my show. Being *known* is being great. No matter what I do to you, the girls *are* gonna want you, and the guys *are* gonna hate your guts with envy."

I was swimming in it now. The lead cannonball in

my stomach had dissolved, and in its place was a launch of balloons like at the start of the Olympics.

"Hell," Matt said as he backed through the door into his booth. "We might even make you mayor."

"Jesus, don't do *that*," I said.

He settled in comfortably at his desk, waited for the song to end, and gave me a brand-new thumbs-up, with a big-brotherly smile. This time I returned salute.

"Okay, constituents, we're back. And our next topic with the candidate will be how the former mayor is enjoying his stay at the federal country club. Fins Foley: life on the *inside*." He drew out the last word suggestively, and pointed to Sol for sound effect. He hit a button and the sound of a howling dog rang in my headphones, screaming, like he was being torn in half.

Was that supposed to be Da, or me?

Flexible Campus was already working exactly the way it was supposed to work. It was designed to give the student a glimpse of the real world and how he was going to fit into it.

I found out, for example, that I was not a night person.

The morning after my first full night at WRRR, I woke for school at eleven o'clock. Who knows how long I would have sacked if my mother hadn't ambled in with an armful of my laundry, all folded and fluffed high with Downy fabric softener, which made my skin break out but which I couldn't stop nuzzling anyway because I was addicted. There, I said it, all right?

"Ahhh!" she shrieked.

"Ahhh!" I shrieked.

As she picked up my things—they'd bounced all over the place with all that Downy spring in them—she scolded me.

"My god, Gordie, I thought you left hours ago."

"Well, Ma, didn't you get suspicious when you didn't see me at the breakfast table?"

"I did so see you there. You ate English muffins

with your father and me. You had three glasses of cranberry juice."

"Oh," I said. I looked under the covers and saw that I was, in fact, dressed for school. "I must have fallen back asleep."

"Oh, do you think so?"

She could be wicked sometimes with the sarcasm.

"Sorry, Ma. Won't happen again. Just getting used to the new hours."

"Yes, well, if you want my vote—"

"I *do*," I snapped reflexively.

"Not that vote. I mean, if you want my opinion, I think the mayor nonsense is probably a better fandango for you than the disc-jockey nonsense. The hours suit you better."

Just then, from out of the dirty pile of laundry she was scooping up, my little flippy phone started its Fisher-Price beepity squeak.

"Jesus," she said, dropping the laundry again.

"Ma, you know, if these chores are getting to be too much for you in your silver years . . ."

Phone buddy blipped again.

"Yes, well, when I'm living in the mayor's mansion with you, I'll be able to lie there like a lump too and watch somebody else do it."

She brought the clothes over and dumped them on me rather than rooting around for the phone herself.

"Hello, Da," I said.

"If that's not the most ridiculous, pretentious little . . ." Ma didn't like the FinsFone much.

"That your ma? Tell her hi for me."

"Da says hi, Ma."

"Hi, Da, don't buy him any more toys, Da," she said on her way out.

"Whoa, wait a minute, Gordie." I heard paper rustling in the background. "What's your ma doing there? Ain't this calculus? I got the schedule you gave me right here in front of me, and it says this is calc period." It did not matter to Da where I was when he called. In fact, I believed he timed the calls for when I would be in a crowd.

"I'm home, Da."

"Why?"

"'Cause I'm a senior. We do shit like that."

"Hmmf. Well. Not anymore you don't. You are a candidate. We have to have you spotless."

"Like yourself," I said, flinching for the oncoming blast.

"Precisely," the prisoner said, meaning it. "Now, Gordie, I gotta ask you some personal questions here, background stuff. There's gonna be a lot of scrutiny on you, and you gotta squeak. We can't wind up embarrassed."

"Hey, Da?" I cut in, not really changing the subject of embarrassment. "You ever listen to the radio?"

"Never. 'Cept the occasional Sox game, and Woo Woo Ginsberg Sunday nights."

"Good. I mean, that's nice."

"Never mind me, here. We have to work on your profile. I want you to go and meet someone. He's going to be sort of your manager, handler. I'll let him do the Q-and-A stuff. He's the best in the business, spin controller supreme. No matter what you look like, this guy'll make you shine. Here's the address. As long as you're playin' hooky—"

"Jesus, Da. *How* old are you? Nobody says 'playin' hooky' anymore."

There was a long silence.

"Gordon," he hummed. "We seem to be getting out of the gate a little early here, in terms of the young colt getting frisky with the old stallion. Ever been kicked in the head by an old gray stallion?"

"What was that address, then?"

"That's my boy. And you do what he says. No smart-mouth."

"None," I said, and hung up. Then, before getting out of bed, I called WRRR and changed my nights to Monday and Wednesday, so I could sleep late on my mayoral days. Perk of the job, I figured.

His name was Bucky, and the address was Bucky's Spuckies Sandwich Shop and Caterer. I knew the man, and the shop, from when I was a kid, though I hadn't been in there in years. It was a quiet little place that I had stared at from the bus a thousand times without really thinking about. Because it was the kind of neighborhood shop you didn't go out of your way to patronize, and my family had left the neighborhood back when everybody else had. But today I noticed it. Because today I wasn't riding the bus, I was navigating the Hawk. And because today Bucky's Spuckies had a new look.

The door opened under a big red sign with the name painted in shock white. To the left of the entrance was a plate-glass window with a menu, pictures of pizza slices and fries to whet the appetite, and, in the middle, a towering cartoon version of a very phallic sub roll in a Superman pose—fists on hips, feet spread wide, cape billowing behind with his BS monogram prominent.

Opposite that window, to the right of the entrance and just as prominent, was a banner. White background, alternating green-and-orange letters, a smattering of shamrocks, and at either end a lion rampant holding the whole thing up.

FOLEY FOR MAYOR

Welcome to campaign headquarters.

"Have a slice, kid. You like a slice?"

I was sitting in a booth with my head in my hands. Bucky had recognized me and come right over. He stood there smiling, one hand in the pocket of his brown double-breasted, the other hand stuck out to me for shaking. Spotless, with polished fingernails, old Buck was most definitely the proprietor here, not the help.

"And some fries. Maybe a steak-and-cheese with some onions, nice, over the top?"

I shook his hand, or rather, was shaken by it.

"No, thanks, can't. Gotta watch the skin. Fins takes an oil sample on my face once a week. If he finds a new zit, he zucks it with his nail clippers."

Bucky laughed heartily, as if there were a video camera recording him. "Sure, then. Let's just get down to beeswax."

"Huh?"

"Hell, I gotta remember how young you are. Beeswax. Business. Like, mind your own beeswax."

I shrugged.

"Okay fine," Bucky huffed. "We'll work on your frame of reference later. Right now, come, let me show you your machine."

My *machine*.

Bucky flipped up the piece of counter that led to the back of the shop, then pushed open the door to Foley Central. He waved his arm over the room, and said, "Here it is, kid, and it's all yours. They do for *you*."

"*This* is cool," I said as I surveyed the operation. "Can they, like, take care of my school election, too? See, I kind of got sucked into running for stupid student body president . . . but frankly I haven't got the time."

Bucky nodded, looked at the personnel. "Don't waste none of your time, Gord. I'll assign somebody right now. Hey you, college boy," he said, waving some guy over.

"Good," the guy piped as he stood up. "*Finally.*" The college boy, just two or three years older than me, with Mr. Peepers specs and straight black hair cut to one length all around his jawline, slapped a pile of envelopes down on the folding card table in front of him. He walked right up to me and pulled something like a baby condom off of his thumb, shoving it in my hand. "Your turn. You're on collating and mass-mailing duty as of now."

Bucky reached out his big hairy mitt and clopped the guy on the side of the head.

"This is the goddamn *candidate*, ya horse's arse. Goddamn college donkey."

Bucky reached out with the other hand for good measure, and clopped him again on the other side.

"Hey," the kid squealed as he recoiled. "You better cut that shit out, Bucky man. I know my rights."

"Ya? And I know your father. And if you don't get some political patronage out of this, he won't pay for your school no more."

"I don't want to hear this," I said, but nobody wanted to hear that.

"Goddamn college monkeys," Bucky snapped, turning to me. "Don't take no shit from any of 'em, Gordie."

Not from any of them. As the specs guy slinked back to his table with his thumb condom, I took in the rest of them. The day shift. Two geezers sitting in front of phones playing checkers. One guy in an apron, with about half a foot of Polish sausage hanging out of his kisser, actually talking on the phone. He wasn't talking about my candidacy, however, unless "I'll bring the ouzo, you bring the ooze," was somehow part of the strategizing. A thirtyish woman in a knee-length dress and mountain-climbing boots ran up to me, blinded me with the flash of her camera, then ran away again backward, as if she were afraid of the ocean and I were a breaker.

It reminded me of the campaign headquarters in *Taxi Driver* and Joe College was nutso Travis Bickle.

"I'm a political-*science* major," he said while madly leafing through a pile of envelopes and slapping computer-generated mailing labels on them.

"That's good, Travis," I said.

"My name is Anthony."

In my pocket, my Batphone rang. Travis-Anthony looked up, surprised. I let it ring again as I stared at him.

"Well, *I* have a flip phone," I said, pointing at myself in case he didn't get it. Bucky excused himself to the kitchen as I picked up.

"Fffoley campaign," I answered, to impress my grandfather as well as my office slaves.

There was nothing but moaning on the line. Exquisite, well-practiced moaning.

"Sweaty." I covered up, walked toward the corner of the room near the drafting table. "Jesus, Sweaty, how did you get this number? Only Fins is supposed to have this number. If he finds you steaming up—"

"Fins gave it to me."

"Bullsh—"

"Wanna know why?"

"I do not. Betty, I'm in the middle of—"

"I visited him."

"Swell."

"He's really very lonely out there."

"Don't."

"I am too, Gordie. Very, very lonely."

"You're just . . . teasing me. You're always like this when I can't get at you. So no, I'm not—"

"I think next time I visit the poor lonely guy I'll ask him for the car. He really likes me—"

"With my bare hands, Sweaty. If you get your meat hooks anywhere near that car—"

Betty was giggling uncontrollably on the other end of the line. "Fine," she said. "I'll let you keep the car, but I do want you to come pick me up."

"For god's sake, Betty, I'm trying to become mayor here. . . ."

"Okay, Gord. I can get somebody else. I think I just saw Marinovich. He's always offering to—"

An involuntary groan slipped out. "Where are you? Don't go *anywhere* in a car with that degenerate Marinovich. Maybe I can get away soon."

"School. Teachers' lounge. But I can't wait forever, Gordie. My best years are, like, wasting away while you play politics."

I slapped the phone shut and jammed it into my pocket. I spun around to find Bucky watching, and listening, with a wry grin on his doughy face.

"Women," he said, like he'd known any.

I nodded.

"She voting age?"

I had to think for a second. "Ah, does it matter?"

Bucky laughed. "Just like the old man," he said.

He gave me the day off.

By the time I burst through the door of the teachers' lounge, she was gone. In her place was the counselor, Vadala, just sitting down with the dregs of the day's last coffee, and Betty's powerful scent. I was getting like a dog, the way I could smell whether she'd been in a spot within the previous six hours, and the way I wanted to roll over and over in that spot.

"Foley," Vadala said brightly. "I sure don't have any trouble remembering you now. Have a seat, boy, you're all sweaty."

"Is she still here? Have you seen her?"

"Who?"

I threw myself down into a chair. Yup, she'd been in it.

"Never mind," I sighed.

"Staying late today?" he asked, and nodded approvingly. "Bravo."

"Truth?" I responded. "Just arriving."

"Oh, my. That's not good."

"Mr. Vadala, I have to tell you . . . it's only the first week of Flexible Campus, and Jesus—"

"Don't thank me, Foley. Hell, if one more senior thanks me for letting him have two cake days a week of working out at the gym or grooming horses . . . What is it with girls and horses, anyway? Can anybody tell me about this?"

"Or running for mayor."

"How's that going, anyway? Pretty exciting I imagine, and educational."

"I imagine."

"Wait, now, aren't you also running for student body president?"

"No," I sighed with fresh new fatigue. "I'm a politician now. *I* am running a political machine, and the *machine* is running for school president. Is there any more of that coffee?"

"The education of a public servant," Vadala said.

"Exactly," the candidate answered.

Mr. Vadala slid me his cup. I took it. I nearly spilled it when the door flung open again and the brown blur, Mr. Coffey, blasted into the room. He was dressed the way he was always dressed, like a UPS driver. Brown polyester pants and shirt, brown shoes.

Coffey was a snapper-pointer. He snapped his fingers, pointed at me, snapped his fingers, pointed at me, etc., rapidly.

Eventually he got it. "Foley, right?"

"Right."

"Mr. Foley's going to be mayor, Mr. Coffey. And student body president," Vadala offered.

"So I hear, so I hear," Coffey replied as he groped at a polyester itch. "Got an awful lot of ambition there, kid."

"He's been storing it up over freshman, sophomore, and junior years, so he's got a surplus." Mr. Vadala winked at me as he said it.

"Heard you on the radio last night," Coffey said.

Why did the sound of that statement make my short hairs prickle? Was not fame the point of all this?

"Your grandfather is, in my opinion"—Coffey paused when his voice broke—"probably one of the ten greatest goddamn Americans of the twentieth century." He misted.

I sighed, relieved and even touched. Fins wasn't making it all up—he sure was beloved by his people.

"So how can you sit there and allow that . . . troglodyte to make jokes about him all night?"

I tensed up again, stomach clenching, palms sweating.

"Time-out here," Vadala said. "Radio? Foley, you were on the radio?"

"It's . . . a little internship thing I got. No big —"

"Yes, and as part of his little internship thing he sits there while a person named Mad Matt says things like, 'Oh, the great irony: What the taxpayers once paid Fins Foley to do to them, they now pay three-hundred-pound convicts to do to Fins.' Well, har-har."

"What?" Vadala was way lost.

"I think you had to be there, Mr. Vadala. It sounded funnier last night."

Coffey stomped to the cooler, blubbed himself a paper cup of water. As he swilled, I waved to Mr. Vadala and slithered out.

When I reached the car, she was there. I could see her from a hundred feet away, bouncing in the seat and jerking the real-wood steering wheel back and forth and back and forth. She looked truly happy and excited, like a little kid, there in the driver's seat. And I knew just what she was doing because I did it myself, all the time: Driving in standstill with the mind doing seventy-five through the wiggly heat vapors on the wide-open road. Just like a little kid.

She jumped when I tapped on the glass. "Hey, hi," she said nervously, straightening her hair in the rearview. As if I'd caught her in the back with a guy or two. She scooted over and I took my rightful place at the wheel of the Gran Tourismo Hawk, and none of it mattered now.

I started to say something, but she stopped me. "Can we just go, Gordie? Driving?" She smiled at me, put her hand on my arm, then smiled at the dash-board.

That was one reason I could love Betty. Because Betty loved the car as senselessly as I did.

A turn of the key and all other stuff wafted up and out in the cloud of blue-brown exhaust smoke. I watched it in the sideview. Gorgeous.

In the morning, early and clear-eyed this time, I was back at headquarters. At the slower speed, in the earlier light, it looked different to me now. It looked more realistic. I saw my position.

I saw it in the window.

FOLEY FOR MAYOR. It was no accident that there was no first name there. It wasn't even a new banner.

I was a stand-in. Which was perfect for me. A lark. But it was dawning on me that the old man didn't quite feel the same way.

"Good to see ya so early, Gordie," Buck said as he opened the front door to me before I was really ready to go in. I went in anyway.

"Pepperoni and egg? Pepperoni and egg. Sure, you'll have one with me. Black pepper, ketchup, and a little sprinkled Romano. *That* is a breakfast, young man."

In his shirtsleeves, Bucky whipped up a couple of fat breakfast subs for us. Then we took the sandwiches out back, to the War Room, as we office-seekers say.

We didn't talk at first, as we both realized how disgusting that would be with the mash of food in our mouths. Instead, I started pawing at the papers spread around. There were drafts of letters to prospective voters introducing me, letters of support from prominent Amberians endorsing me even though they'd never met me, and there was the flier. A one-page sheet with some background information about my family (true enough), my Boy Scout achievements (greatly embellished), and my community service (news to me). But this was all standard stuff that we could have produced in our seventh-grade mock election in current-events class. What I did find interesting was common to every single piece of literature. Very lightly, ghostlike, in the background of every piece of campaign literature like a watermark, was the silhouette of the 1963 Studebaker Gran Tourismo Hawk. Top down, of course. My car, but, more importantly, for the last two decades or so, Fins Foley's trademark.

So, not only had the car stolen my girlfriend from me, it was running for mayor.

I was so pissed off. I could have . . .

Jesus, though, look at that car. Who could stay mad at it?

"Jesus, Bucky," I said, even though pepperoni and stuff was spilling from my mouth. "Will you just look at it. Wouldja?"

"Jesus, I know," he said, and he did know, though

I hadn't even pointed at it or spoken its name or anything. Chilling.

Power.

The Hawk had it.

Maybe I could borrow some.

"Oh, you hear that, folks? Can you beeee-lieve our boy here?" Mad Matt was on a rave. "And they say there are no Thomas Jeffersons anymore. They say there are no Leonardo da Vincis. No more Renaissance men? Phuoa!" Matt spat into his microphone, not for real, but an impressive simulation of expectoration. "All right, he's running for mayor of our fine city; he's running for student body president; *and*, I don't mind telling you, he's practically running the whole show here at WRRR, because Sol over there, he's all but useless. Am I right, Sol? The kid's gone beyond candidate already, beyond heroic. We're sit-ting here with a demigod, is what we're doing, *only* at station WRRR. The other guys have *no* demigods on staff.

"So, like, what about a social life, there, Gordie? Is there a special someone?"

I hedged. Forgot where the button was to open my microphone. Matt made a *duh* face at me. I located the switch.

"Sweaty Betty," I blurted.

"Sweat—?" Matt interrupted himself. Then he hummed deliciously into the microphone. "Could we hear that again, Mr. Mayor?"

"Ah, her name is Betty."

"The other part."

"Sweaty Betty."

"Ohhh, lllordy. Children, children, children," he gushed. I thought he was going to leap on top of his desk. Matt pointed quickly at Sol, who snapped in a tape. "Howww fortuitous," Matt sang, while in the background Eddie Murphy also sang. That is, Murphy as Buckwheat sang the Supremes' "Reach Out and Touch Somebody's Hand."

"Yes, that's right, all you politicos and politicas, it is time for the 'Reach Out and Touch' portion of our program. In a few minutes we'll be back with Amber's future First Lady, Sweaty Betty. Meanwhile, kick back with the newest hit from Felonious Fins Foley, a tune called 'It's My Party, and I'll Squeal Like a Pig If I Want To.' "

I wanted to say no. In fact, I attempted it.

"Ah, I'm sorry, what was that?" Matt asked.

I tried again.

"Come again? I didn't catch that." He had his hand cupped behind his ear. Sol was finally laughing at something. We had variations on this exchange two more times. Each time, Matt's delivery was a little less funny, and Sol laughed a little harder.

"I *told* the people we were calling her, Gordie.

Were you listening? Did you *hear* me tell the people?"
He had the look and the low rumble dogs get when
they stop making the big noise just before they bite.

I gave him the number. She'd probably love it anyway. Probably? Of course she'd love it. That's what I
was afraid of.

"Hello? Hey, yes, is Sweaty there?"

Well, naturally, it was her father who answered.
On the air, to boot, since Matt always worked without
a net.

"All right, punk, which one are you. Robert? This
you again, Robert?"

"No sir, Mr. Sweaty. My name is Matt, and I'm
on—"

"Matt. Marinovich? You filthy little pervert, I told
you if you ever called my daughter again—"

Robert? Robert had been calling my Betty? And
Marinovich? Yeeesh.

"No, sir, listen, this is Mad Matt of radio station
WRRR. And I'm here with Gordie Foley, future—"

"Gordie? Hey, hey, Gordie, how the hell are ya?"

Betty's father and I had never spoken. Not once.
She told me boys were not allowed to call her, and
never, never were they allowed to come to the house.
The guy was a total rumor to me. I didn't know what
I was to him.

"Gordie," he said again when I didn't answer, out
of fear. "This is you, right? Betty's new boyfriend,
Gordon Foley?"

New. Betty and I had dated, more or less, for about two years now.

"Hey, Mr. Hansen," I said. "Can we speak to Betty, please?"

"Hell, I couldn't even believe it when she told me the other day, she was dating somebody famous like you."

The other day? Two *@#% years, and she just told him *the other day*? It was like I was a pod creature and I'd just popped into existence when . . . well, we all know when, don't we?

"Boy, when are we going to have you over to supper?"

Maybe he was the pod.

Matt was frantic on the other side of the glass, wheeling his arm like he was waving me in from third. Sol jabbed me in the neck with a pen.

"Ah, Saturday. Can I talk to Betty now?"

"Saturday, then. Sure you can talk to her." He dropped the phone loudly, then picked it up again. "Be sure to bring the car, now."

"Sure," I sighed.

"Hey, hey, am I on?" Sweaty Betty cooed.

"Sure sounds like it to me," Mad Matt answered, rubbing his hands together hard enough to start a fire.

"Hey, Betty," I said meekly.

"Hey, loverboy," she said, just to make me squirm.

"So tell me do, Sweaty—by the way, that's a lovely name you've got there."

"Thank you, Mad. I got it way back in the fifth grade. One day I came to school without—"

"You don't have to tell him that," I jumped in.

"Hush, Gordie," she said.

"Ya," Matt added. "Hush now, Gordie. Don't worry, Betty, you'll have your chance to tell us all about yourself later. Right now we want to ask you about the demigod here. Is he as amazing as he seems to the rest of us?"

She paused. Let out a rapturous, loud, juicy sigh. "Yes, Matt, he is."

"Well, how is it then? With all he's got going at the moment, has he got anything left for . . . you know, for you? Or are you another political widow?"

"Let me just tell you, Matt, about this savage beast of a candidate—"

"Honey . . ." I said through gritted teeth. "You don't have to answer anything you don't want to—"

"I want to," she chirped.

"Say good-bye for a while, Gordie. Gordie's going on break for a while, folks. He'll be back later in the show," Matt said, and made a slashing motion across his throat. Sol did something at the board, grinned, and I was temporarily off the air.

"Bye, sweetie," Sweaty twittered. I listened in silence as she told impressive, totally fabricated stories of my manliness.

It was one thirty when I got home after my shift. My mother was sitting at the kitchen table in her flannels, with red-rimmed eyes. She didn't even slow down when I came in. She had a mission to complete before she dealt with me, and that mission was to finish the entire box of little yellow marshmallow Easter chicks that had been in the back of the pantry for six months. There, done.

"You *told* me it was an off-the-air internship," she said in the practiced calm voice that was, in effect, the anticalm voice.

"Mother." I thought it best to go right into an aggressive, scolding mode. "You told me you never listen to that show."

"Right. But your cousin Matthew does. And he told his mother, who naturally called me. As did Carol's mother. As did Hannah and Conor's mother. As did Charles's mother. As did—"

I shrugged. "If you ground me, I can't run my campaign."

"You're eighteen," she sighed. "We're not going to ground you anymore."

"Cool," I said. The first good words of the night.

She pointed at me menacingly. "But I'm *not* going to vote for you."

Which, apparently, was what she needed to say to let off the steam. She pushed herself up from the table, noticed her fingers sticking, and licked the tips as she walked past me. I turned to follow her, then wrapped my arms around her and squeezed as we waddled out of the kitchen together.

"Oh, you are so going to vote for me," I said into her ear.

"Hmmmph," she responded, which meant yes. "But does she have to call herself that name for the whole world to hear?"

W hen I went back to work at campaign headquarters, I was towing the beginnings of an entourage. "Jackie! Jackie Foley, how are you?" Bucky gushed, scooting to the door to meet her.

"I'm fine, Bucky," Ma answered primly. She was surveying the office. She was not smiling. "Are you telling me Fins used this place all those years as his headquarters?"

Bucky shrugged. "Fins always was a populist, Jackie. Man of the little—"

"Pffft," she snorted. "Well I never voted for that one, and I'm not voting for this one." She was thumb-jerking in the direction of me, her only child.

"Yes she is," I countered.

"Never?" Bucky was astounded. "You *never* voted for Fins?"

She shook her head proudly. "I love my father-in-law. But he was a lousy, fat, irresponsible blowhard of a frivolous, spendthrift, self-satisfied politician. *Not* the finest qualifications for a mayor."

"But the *very* finest qualifications for a grandfather," I answered.

Bucky laughed. Ma did not.

"So then why are you here?" Bucky asked, pulling out a chair for her.

"I'm here to help my son. I may not support Gordie the public figure, but I do support Gordie the boy. Even if I'm not going to vote for him."

"She's gonna vote for me." I winked at Bucky.

"This is beautiful," Bucky said, wiping a non-existent tear from his eye.

"Cut the nonsense, Bucky," Ma snapped, "and get me some envelopes to stuff."

Bucky saluted her army-style and scurried to get her some work.

"So," I said, clasping my hands in front of me. "Does this mean I get to boss you around? Send you out for coffee and toilet paper and all the other supplies my workers use so much of?"

"You just try it," she said, shimmying out of her jacket.

Bucky plunked himself down in the seat across the card table from me. "Have you ever done drugs?" Bucky asked, very businesslike, licking the tip of his pen.

I did not answer. Looked over my shoulder at my mother, who was working envelopes the way a monkey works peanuts. She had one way-arched eyebrow aimed at me.

"Buuuuuuck?" I whispered. "What are you doing to me? That's my *mother*."

"Listen," he said, laying his pen down across his

yet-unsoiled page. "If you got stuff to say that your mom can't hear, we got some troubles, imagewise."

Beeeeep. The FinsFone.

"Foolish thing," mother opined.

"Hey, Da."

"How come I ain't been faxed yet? I was supposed to be reading the candidate's profile with my All Bran this morning."

"Guess the bread-and-water thing's kind of a myth, huh?"

"Put Bucky on."

"We're working on it right now, Fins. Ya, coming along just fine. You were right, the kid's immaculate, not a blemish on his history."

"Pshhhh," Ma interjected from her gallery-of-one. "Even *I* know that's not true."

"Ya, that's Jackie," Bucky said. "*Gung*-ho to work for the boy. She's a dynamo, gonna make all the difference for us."

"Are you *incapable* of telling the truth?" Ma asked my manager.

"Let him do his job, Ma," I bossed. Felt good. I could warm up to this.

Bucky folded up the phone and handed it back to me. I tucked it into the inside pocket of my dungaree jacket. He looked pensive.

"What?" I asked.

"Your grandfather, he has an . . . idealized view of you, I think."

"That's my da," I chirped.

"But is he *right?*" Bucky demanded.

"Ah, ya. Well, ya, pretty much. In *spirit*, I think, he knows me pretty well, which is important, I think."

Bucky began shaking his head gravely. "Two things, all right? First, if you're gonna be any good at this whatsoever, we have to train you to lie better than that. Second, if it takes you that long to answer every one of my questions, it's gonna take us all day, and we ain't got all day. I gotta start calling newspapers about you, we got a handful of new college volunteers I gotta train on the phones this afternoon—"

"New college recruits, huh? Any of them girls, Bucky?"

"I think a few, ya, but forget about that. Serious now. We have work to do. I want this bio shit ready for next week, which is gonna be your first fund-raiser. A hundred-and-fifty-dollar-a-plate affair."

"A buck fifty *a plate?* Jesus, Bucky, what's on the plate, cocaine?"

He put his pen down again.

"Gordie." He paused, sighed, ran his hands back over his head. Tried it again. "Gordie. Conditions . . . are such that this whole thing, the campaign, will run quite smoothly of its own power. Unless . . ." He raised an emphatic finger. "Unless you, the candidate, say or do something asinine."

I smiled at him. Hoping to relieve some of the gathering tension. The tension resisted my smile.

"And it is becoming apparent, Gordon, that you are quite capable of just such a thing."

I waited what I thought was an appropriate amount of time before speaking.

"I'm a senior," I said. I shrugged.

Bucky slid the form across the table to me. "You fill it out, Gordie. Bring it back to me when you return on Thursday. In the meantime I'll run the campaign, and you keep from derailing it. Cool?"

"Cool," I said.

"You're free to go."

"Now? What about the girls?"

"I'll tell your mom to look them over and get back to you."

The next day was Wednesday. A school day, a sweet, simple school day like they all used to be, cruising the halls unknown and unperturbed. No demands, no expectations, no image making, no politics.

Then again, maybe not.

"Where have you been?" Mosi snapped. He was sitting on the windowsill at the back of homeroom. I was five minutes ahead of the bell, as usual. Mosi was way early, for him.

"I've been in bed, then I've been at the kitchen table, then I've been in the car—"

"We have work to do."

"No we don't, Mos. We're seniors." I slapped him on the arm to reassure him.

For a second he looked reassured. Then he shook it off. "No, Gordie, we have to work on your campaign. We're way behind."

"Please, not you too. I feel like I'm working on that stupid thing twenty-four hours a day. I was kind of hoping school would be a break."

"No can do, man. If we want to win, we have to catch up right now."

I slid down into my chair. I was starting to feel constantly now as if it was time to brush my teeth and hit the sack, no matter what time of day it was.

"Mosi, I have to tell you, I'm starting to doubt whether this is even worth scoring a great car and all the delicious chickens in town."

Mosi slapped me. Like General Patton in the movie.

I sat there, stunned. Then the insanity of my words registered.

"Thanks, man," I said. "I'm ready to work."

I hopped up onto the windowsill next to him and pulled my mayoral questionnaire out of my back pocket. "Actually, I was planning to ask you for a little help with this anyway. This mayor shit is getting complicated."

Mosi stared at it, then pulled something out of his own back pocket.

"No, no, no, I don't mean that," he said. "I mean this."

It was a copy of our imaginative school newspaper, *The School Newspaper*. Top story was the result of the paper's student-body-president poll.

"There was a poll? How did I not even know there was a poll?"

"One might say you're out of touch, prez. Read on."

I read, out loud. " 'Maureen McCormack, forty percent.' " I turned to Mosi. "Do I know her? Wait, she's a junior, right? Black hair, like, six feet tall?"

"Close. She was in *The Brady Bunch*."

" 'Ollie North, twenty-two percent. Him, I know. 'Robert O'Dowd, eighteen percent.' " I gave this one more considered thought. "He was that freaky guy in *The Crying Game*."

"No. O'Dowd's real. Football tricaptain."

"I see. 'Tracy Bannon, sixteen percent.' Ohhhh. I know Tracy. She's real."

"Quite."

"Okay, and down here on the bottom, we have . . . 'Other, four percent.' 'Other?' "

"I checked. There were a couple of freshmen that voted for themselves, a write-in for the bacon-burger lady in the cafeteria who only speaks Portuguese, and you."

"Well," I said calmly, practicing my new think-before-speaking policy. "That's not very good. But the question is, do I give a rat's ass?"

"I don't know, Gord, do you?"

"Let me check. . . . No, I don't think so. Mos,

remember, I just backed into this thing because I didn't want to get beat up by Sweaty for talking to those girls. Who, other than a complete putzball, would want to spend the greatest year of his life kissing asses to be elected head dildo of this peckerhead factory?"

"Wow." Mosi hopped down from the sill as the bell rang to go to first period. "Now that you put it that way . . . you're getting to be some kind of a persuasive orator since you've been running for mayor."

I hopped down and started walking with him. "I know it. The whole experience is, like, changing me. It's a lot of things . . . the Gran Tourismo Hawk, the radio gig, my own personal campaign office with college girls working for me and stuff."

"College girls?"

"Ya, you wanna volunteer?"

"Can you make 'em do whatever you say, 'cause you're the candidate?"

"Don't know. I haven't tried it out yet. But I figure it must be like being a really good guitarist in a really hot band, you know. It's got to make you look prime no matter what kind of a melon you are. I'm feeling all nuts and buzzy with power these days."

"Wow some more. I'm volunteering, then."

"Done. First thing is, meet me at lunch to try and work out this questionnaire thing. It's gonna be a bitch, from what I can tell."

"I'll be there."

"And keep next Thursday night open. Get this—

there's a hundred-and-fifty-dollar-a-plate fund-raiser for me at some club."

"A hundred and . . . what's on the plate, cocaine?"

"See, now that's what *I* said."

The phone rang as Mosi headed to his class. I let it ring a few more times so that I could feel the way all the hall-crossers were looking at me. Other than the drug dealers', mine was the only body in school that rang.

"Hey, Da," I said, clanging against a yellow locker.

"I want to see you. This afternoon," he grrred.

And all the nuts-and-buzzy power seeped out of me just like that, leaving me shrunk down to what I used to be.

"Hello, Da," I said easily, poking my head into the room.

He said nothing at first. He was sitting in his usual chair, casually leafing through a paper. The guard—he waved to me—was standing by the rear door.

"Cross-country team's doing very well. Football team still stinks, unfortunately." He turned a page, working the paper from back to front. "Oh good, they've needed to renovate those lavatories for a long time now, haven't they." He was quickly to the front page. It was only an eight-pager. "What do you know . . . old Ollie North. Never gives up, does he? I have to remember to give him a call."

Fins slapped the newspaper down in his lap and glowered at me.

"Oh. Well hello there . . . *Other*. I didn't even realize you were here. Funny, how some people can be there, and then again seem like they're not."

"It's not my fault, Da. And I never said I was the most popular guy in the school."

"Most popular? Gordie, you're off the chart. You're a flippin' asterisk."

"Can I ask you how you got that, my dinky little school paper, here in . . . I mean, you subscribe, or what?"

"You may not ask. Gordie, we can't have this. You're a Foley."

"If you don't mind my saying so, Da . . . who gives a shit? It's crappy old student body president, which I don't even want anyhow."

"Ya, well it's too late for that. You know what the real papers will do with this? You wanna be mayor, but you come in goddamn twelfth in your own high school. . . ."

"No, wait a minute. *I* don't wanna be mayor. *You* want me to be mayor. And you promised I don't really have to win, remember?"

He waved me off. "Image, Gordie. Image, is what we're talking about. You know and I know and everybody in this town with half a brain—which our research shows is like forty percent of 'em—knows that it ain't you runnin' for mayor, it's me. See, I had my successor picked, and everybody could see that she was gonna be me. Then she started not working out. So my boy, my grandson, my Gordie, he shows up with his perfect Foley face, he's in the race, and my loyal constituency, they get the signal. You wanna vote for Fins—which most of 'em want to do—you vote for Gordie."

I started panicking. "I gotta *win*? I *knew* it, you tricked me, Da. Jesus Christ." I started flapping my arms and pacing like a zoo gorilla. "I had other plans, Da. This was my big year. I'm already way more popular than I can handle—"

"At four percent?"

"And now what you're telling me is I couldn't lose if I wanted to. Which I do. How can I go on the Bermuda trip with the rest of the class if I gotta be stupid goddamn mayor, huh? How can I moon at halftime of the Thanksgiving Day game like everybody else?"

Fins was now waving his own hands, telling me to whoa.

"You don't gotta win. Remember, we just need to scare your opponent back on course. She'll be fine. And, no offense, but I need her. She's good. You . . . might have some difficulty with the day-to-day that I couldn't do for ya."

"Damn right I would."

I stood there hyperventilating, but with nothing left to argue. Fins knew what he was doing. He always knew . . . except with those undercover FBI guys; but, live and learn.

"So," he said smoothly, back in charge. "We gotta fix this school thing. It's an embarrassment. And as beloved as I am, there are some people who wouldn't mind having some mean fun at the old man's expense."

I sighed. At least I didn't have a seizure this time.

"That's right, kid. I'm afraid the school, you're gonna have to win."

"Da, I'm sorry to let you down, but I don't know if that's possible."

He folded up his little newspaper and tucked it under his arm. Then he stood and shuffled away toward the door.

"It's possible," he said. "Go now, run along and play. Be young. Enjoy yourself."

For once, we had the same idea.

I watched his hunched shoulders as he faded through the door. And I noticed that my legendary grandfather was looking like a little old man.

D inner with the buck-fifty–plate club turned out to be more complicated than which-spoon-is-for-the-fruit-cup. Bucky warned me that I was going to have to do a little speech thing. And even though he threatened to pull me right off the podium by my tie—a *tie?*—if I spoke for more than eight minutes, that was about seven minutes beyond what I figured my material required. So I had to prepare that. And there was still the questionnaire thing.

"You have to help me, Mos."

"I don't know, Gordie," he answered grimly. "Four percent. I mean, you *shared* four percent. Even I didn't realize you were that unpopular."

We were sitting in Mosi's garage among component rubble. He had dismantled four of his guitars for no apparent reason, scrambled up the strings, pickups, tuning keys, knobs, switches, etc., and was attempting to reassemble them in bold new ways.

"I'm a visionary, you know," he said as he stared, vacant and glassy-eyed, at the pile of stuff. "I could do something radical here."

"What exactly were you after here, Mos?"

He started giggling. "I'm a visionary. How the hell should I know?"

He picked up an intact guitar from the arrangment of guitars left standing, and he started to strum. Standing right on the pile of loose components.

"So what does all this mean, Mosi, that because you found out I'm behind in the poll you're not going to help me?"

"I didn't say that."

"No? So what did you say?"

Mosi opened his mouth, stopped strumming, pointed at me with his pick, then giggled some more. "I don't know, Gord. What did I say?"

I snapped at him. "You are the most useless—"

"Can we go to Burger King?"

"What?"

"I'm starving."

"Jesus, Mosi. Are you listening to me? This isn't funny anymore. I, like, have all this pressure on me all of a sudden, and I have to produce. It's as if nobody gives a shit that this is my senior year at all."

He stared at me with St. Bernard eyes. Hopeless.

"You buying?" I sighed.

He shook his head.

"Jesus Christ, Mosi. What good—"

"Don't you have an expense account?"

"As a matter of fact, I do," I said. Fins had given me one of his gold cards, which I never used, but would let slip out of my wallet when delicious chickens were around to see it. He also had been feeding me cash through Bucky. "But my expense account is only to be spent on volunteers and campaign-related incidentals."

"Ah," he probed, "am I in there somewhere?"

I pulled out my questionnaire. "Can you show me how to do some of that big-ass lying you do?"

He smiled, put the guitar back on its stand, and led me out by the arm. "I have never told more than an innocent white lie, and even then it was only to help out a desperate friend."

"Ya," I said, "that's it. Just like that."

At Burger King, Mosi ordered three cheeseburgers, onion rings, curly fries, and a chicken-tenders kids' meal. In the kids' meal he received a little Disney Pocahontas figurine.

"First off, have I ever done drugs?"

Both of his cheeks were puffed with food. He held up one finger for me to wait while he masticated. I hate waiting when a guy does that.

He swallowed, held the figurine up high. "I think Pocahontas is maybe the finest Disney babe yet."

"Stop it, Mos, we got work here."

"Mmmm," he said, staring and thinking some more. "No *maybe*. She is the finest. Look at those eyes."

"You're just trying to provoke me. Cut it out."

"No, man. I'm in love."

I slammed down my pen. This had to stop right here.

"You have no taste, Mosi, you know that? Pocahontas is maybe *half*—and I'm being generous—maybe half the woman Jasmine is."

"Forget about it. You don't know what you're talking about. Forget the eyes, okay. Let's talk about the buckskin, and the Wonderbra she's gotta have on under it."

"Oh, time out. You can't count attire. That's not part of the scoring. If it was, how about Ariel? All right, seashells. The girl wears nothing but a pair of seashells. If that isn't fineness—"

"I forgot about the shells. And don't forget, Gordie, she loses her voice partway through the movie. A girl who wears seashells *and* can't talk . . . I change my vote. It's Ariel."

He had me pondering. As usual, I was pondering all the wrong things.

"Drugs, Mosi! The question was, have I ever tried drugs?"

"Oh," he said, like he'd just walked in. "Is that all? Well, the answer is yes."

"No, no, no, the answer is *not* yes."

"It's not?"

"No, it's not. I am a candidate for public office, don't you see? I've got to approach this carefully. See, if they drug-test me, I'm clean, that's not an issue. But if they go digging around asking questions . . ."

"Gotcha. So the answer is no."

Poor Mosi. He sounded so proud, too.

"Wrong. They'll think I'm lying because I'm a teenager and they figure we're *all* stoned. So I have to come up with just *the* answer, which makes me look a little bit hip, but not hip enough to be threatening, and honest. Honest is good. Is there such an answer?"

As I spoke, I had gotten so involved in the dilemma that I was rubbing my hands together and staring at them, ignoring Mosi entirely. When I looked up again, he was in the process of fitting one whole cheeseburger in his mouth at once and staring at Pocahontas again. His eyes were a glaze.

I wrote him off, folded my arms across the table, and tucked my face into the crevice there.

"You didn't inhale," he said calmly after swallowing.

I raised my head. "What did you say?"

"You tried smoking dope on two occasions. But you did not inhale."

I beamed at him, and in his reflective face the pride was back. "Mosi. Mosi, you stud. That's so damn stupid, it's genius. It's the perfect wishy-washy, please-everybody-and-don't-actually-say-a-damn-thing answer imaginable," I said, and started scribbling. "I don't know how you do it, Mos."

"Neither do I. I just get, like, visions sometimes."

"Cool. Let me know when you get another one."

"Okay. How 'bout this: With the pills, you only licked 'em."

"No, Mos. I think we have enough here."

"And with the needle—"

"Mosi! Thank you. That'll do, thanks. I think we got it covered. Here, here's two bucks, go get a cherry pie."

He got the pie, came back, and sat down as I finished writing.

"Do you think they'll be interested in your thing for fabric softener?"

"I don't think it'll come up, Mos. Okay, next," I said. "Do I attend church regularly?"

"Jesus, they're tough," he said.

"Tell me about it," I concurred. "It gets worse, even. Wait'll you see."

"He's here. He's back. He's hot as a pistol. Dead last in the student-body-president race, but numero uno in our hearts—boys and girls, give it up for Gordie 'Little Fins' Foley."

Mad Matt flipped some switches, cued Sol to do likewise, blew a party horn, and basically did all that jackass stuff he was great at.

"Hi, everyone," I said, so quietly that Matt had to signal me to speak up. "This week's report is, yes, it appears that I am starting slowly in the school race—"

"*Slowly?*" Matt jumped in. He had a control where he could not only talk over me, he could shut my mike off completely while he did it. "Slowly? Gordie, the *Titanic* started slowly. For you they would have just built the ship right there on the bottom of the ocean."

"I'm building some momentum," I countered with no conviction. "And secondly, I don't care for the name 'Little Fins.' "

"You don't. All right, I admit, it wasn't my best work, but some days. . . Wait a minute." Matt's face lit up. His voice rose and he got up out of his chair. "Where do we always turn when we are in need?"

Shit, I thought. It's gonna be a long night. Sol was laughing already, which he was now doing with more regularity than he had in the history of the show.

"To our loyal and insightful listeners, of course. So pick up your phones, kiddies, and join in the great American political process. Let your voice be heard as we play the all-important Name the Candidate game! Help the boy out, gang. It's no wonder he's getting drubbed. Can't be a decent candidate without a gripping handle."

"I like Gordie," I tried.

There was a loud buzzing sound effect that blasted my eardrums. "Nope, sorry, Gord. Doesn't rhyme."

Sweaty was the first to call. "How 'bout Gord the Sword," she moaned. She sounded like a 900 number.

"Would you please get off the line," I snapped. "This is hard enough."

"I bet," she added before clicking.

The Hawk, for all its greatness, is definitely no more than a four-passenger vehicle. This worked out well for the fund-raiser because I wound up squiring not only my volunteer/nonsupporter mother and her date, my nonvolunteer/nonsupporter father, but also my visionary assistant, Mosi. Sweaty refused to come after I told her to shut up over the public airwaves. She insisted on an apology over those same airwaves, and since I wouldn't have the chance until tomorrow night, no Sweaty tonight.

Anyway, I had Mosi. My parents hopped into the backseat together, and let Mosi ride up front like he was my date. He was wearing a maroonish suit that clung to his big short arms and thick neck like he was growing right out of it before our eyes. And though we were on our way to dinner, he came packing a gigantic bag of Smartfood.

As I warmed up the Tourismo in the driveway—regardless of the weather, you let her idle for exactly four minutes or you are abusing her—Mos sat in the passenger seat, bearing down on the popcorn like a horse with a feedbag.

"What's up with you?" I asked, whispering a little bit lower than my folks were whispering and giggling in back. I turned on the radio, but nothing would come out of it until the tubes heated up.

"Nuth," he garbled.

"Look at me, Mosi."

He looked up. Popcorn cheese ringed his mouth

and sprinkled his eyebrows like fairy dust. The eyes themselves were dewy and unfocused. I sniffed him.

"Jesus Christ," I snapped.

"What is it?" my father asked.

The radio, warmed, blasted in out of nowhere. The four minutes was not quite up, but I threw the car in reverse, apologizing to it as I did.

"Nothing, Dad. Mosi just has popcorn cheese on his suit, and he looks like a *dick*!" I snarled.

"Gordon!" Ma gasped. Dad and Mosi seemed not to mind.

"Want some Smartfood?" Mosi asked, swinging around and aiming the bag at my parents.

I swiped the bag out of his hand, threw it out the window. "No eating in the Studebaker. I told you this a million times."

"A little nervous about tonight, son?" Ma asked.

I grunted.

"What's that sound? What's that sound I hear back there?" I was just asking for dramatic effect. I knew very well what the sound was, just as I knew the Hawk's every sound. It was the creaking of the tiny spring that holds down the lid on the mini-ashtray in the rear door handle. "There's no smoking in the Studebaker, Dad. You know that."

I watched his laugh lines in the mirror. He was enjoying himself. "Used to be able to smoke in the Studebaker," he said, grandly draping his arm over my mother's shoulders.

What is it about this car that makes guys do that?

"In fact," he reminisced, "everybody did. My dad would be tooling along in the front seat on a Sunday afternoon, one arm around my mom, beeping and waving at everybody we passed. He really was king back then, I'll give him that. Anyhow, he'd have a big old stogie stuck in his kisser, Mom would be smoking a tiparillo—she was a maverick herself—and me and my sister would be all scrunched down in back sharing a butt out of the ashtray."

Dad paused to laugh at his story. "With the top down, and all the parade-waving they did, my folks never even knew what we were doing back there. Everybody in town saw us smoke except our own damn parents, heh-heh." There was an extra little twist to that last laugh that was kind of chilling.

"Awesome story, Mr. Foley," Mosi doofed.

"Ya, really cool, Dad. But you still can't smoke now. Times have changed. New regime. Get with the program."

He booed me. I was a high-school kid, last in the poll, on his way to make a speech to adults with money. My date, who was *not* pretty enough to get away with it, smelled like a Rastafarian priest. And my very father was booing me.

"It's called preaching to the converted," Bucky said, in an effort to calm me down. "It's the easiest thing in the world. You don't have to win anybody over. This is your grandfather's core of support, his inner circle. They love him, they love you. And all two hundred of 'em have paid a buck fifty apiece to prove it."

"Two hun . . . at a hundred fif . . ."

Bucky stood patiently, waiting for me to defeat the equation. He couldn't wait any longer.

"Gord, has anyone mentioned to you that the mayor has to manage a one-hundred-*million*-dollar budget?"

"Jesus, I wish people would stop saying that to me."

"Forget it. Just go out there and accept the people's love. Tell a joke, do some rah-rah, talk about your dear da. Then get down before you put your foot in it."

"Thanks, coach," I said.

I worked up a full greasy sweat at dinner, mumbling to myself like a psychopath as I practiced sounding natural. Fifty different people came by to introduce themselves as lifelong FOFs (Friends Of Fins), and I established my credibility as a politician by slipping every one of them the slimiest handshake of his life. My father laughed at almost everything because he, unlike his son, had not lost the ability to not take any of it seriously. I had to stop looking at my mother after a while because the pain became too great. She saw the anguish in my face, which brought her to the brink of tears, which, when I saw that, brought me to

the brink of tears, and so on. Mosi ate his chicken cor-
don bleu in three bites, ate his baked potato and its
skin, and some of its foil wrapper. He ate the wrinkled
peas, the garnish, and the lemon slice in his water.

"You gonna finish that?" he asked me.

My food was untouched. "Mosi, first why don't you
ask me if I'm going to *start* it?"

"You gonna start—"

I shoved my plate toward him.

" . . . *Gordon . . . Foley!*" That was all I heard.
There must have been an intro of some kind because
I had a vague recollection of Bucky's voice over the
P.A., but nothing registered until I heard my name,
and the terrifying applause that followed it.

I toddled up the two steps to the podium and settled in under the four-foot-by-six-foot photo of my
grandfather, smiling broadly and waving, cigar in fingers, from the driver's seat of *my* car. So why wasn't *he*
up here doing the dirty work, I thought. Anyway, I
was happy to see half the room still concentrating on
eating, receiving desserts, trading tastes, flagging wait-
resses for more coffee. So I just said hi and launched,
hoping my seven minutes would evaporate before they
noticed me.

"So when Bucky told me . . . a hundred and fifty
dollars a plate, just to come and listen to *me* . . ." I
paused. My comic timing, at least, was functioning. "I
asked him, 'What's on the plate, Buck, cocaine?' "

I had thought, previously, that silence was one of

those absolute things, that there were not *degrees* of silence. But this, this *thing*, this fearsome black nothing of silence, was a new experience in my eighteen years. Not even a fork grazing a plate.

That was, of course, until Mosi caught up to us.

"*Bar-har-ar-har-ar-har* . . ." and so on. His laugh, zipping through the still room, bouncing off this wall and that one, back again, crisscrossed the room several times, slicing me every which way like a *Star Wars* laser.

Despite what common sense tells him, a guy just has to look to his mother at a time like that. I was actually relieved to find her finally crying, in a controlled, dignified way. Now it was behind us, and I could slog through. My father held her hand, with the other hand cupped over Mosi's mouth, and nodded for me to continue.

I looked over to Bucky, who was doing a mime version of driving a car. Pause. Comprehension.

"Well, what I really just want to tell you is, when you see me behind the wheel of that car . . ."

Bucky mimed a shark now, weaving through the imaginary water, his hand sticking up like a divider in the middle of his head. Oh ya, mention Da, mention Da.

"*Fins*, Fins's car. When you see me in Fins's car, you should know that it's not just a coincidence. It's not just appearance. It's a tradition. This symbolizes continuity, a carrying on of the tradition of fine service the Foley family has provided the people of Amber for decades. The spirit of populism, our commitment to all the little men and women of our city—will not diminish in the transition from one Foley to the next."

There was a nice swelling of polite, sincere, relieved applause from the crowd. Bucky did the shark-fin thing again.

"Oh, so, remember, if you loved Fins Foley as mayor—and who didn't?"—laughs, claps—"you're going to love Gordie Foley. The common man's new best friend."

I checked my watch, and realized that I was quite short of my seven minutes. I looked up to find Bucky frantically waving me down off the podium anyway. I waved, and left. That brought the big applause.

As I stepped down, Bucky rushed to meet me. He smiled and shook my hand excitedly, then leaned close to my ear. "Please don't say any more refreshing things. They're going to kill us."

I shook hands, shook hands, took a beer that was offered me without thinking. Bucky, escorting me from table to table, snatched it out of my hand. "Thank you very much," he said to the nice man who'd given it to me. "He'll drink it three years from now, when it's legal." Laughs, laughs.

"This," said Bucky with unusual respect, "is a very good friend of your grandfather's, Mr. Saltonstall."

Mr. Saltonstall stood up, a lanky and elegant white-haired guy about six three. I wiped my hand off on my pants leg and shook.

"A pleasure, Gordon," he said. "Have a seat."

I took the vacant seat at the circular table next to Mr. Saltonstall. Then he gave Bucky a look that quickly got rid of Bucky. Then others from his group quietly slipped away.

"Manager wouldn't let you have the beer, huh?"

I shook my head, feeling now like the kid that I was.

Mr. Saltonstall reached across the table and grabbed the neck of the orange-label champagne bottle. He poured two long, tall, dainty glasses and handed me one.

"My parents are here, though," I said.

"I know. Your father sipped champagne while sitting on my *knee* at one of these a long, long time ago."

"Wow," I said, and turned to check out my parents' reaction. My dad nodded and blinked just slightly, like at an auction. Mosi pumped his fist.

"I'm proud to see you doing this, Gordon," Mr. Saltonstall said. "And I love your grandfather."

I sipped. "Everybody does," I said.

"I believe that's true. And I'll bet this all makes for a pretty heady senior year of high school, am I right?"

I sighed, took a longer sip.

"How are you holding up? Anything you need to make it easier? Anything, you just let me know."

"I could use another glass of champagne," I said, smiling. He poured it.

"I just wanted you to know, Gordie, how much all

of us in this room feel for Fins. And that this"—he made a sweeping gesture over the full gathering of people—"is more or less our testimonial to that. To him."

I looked around the room, which was full of Fins's people, his old friends, supporters, cronies. I noticed that even though they were all mingling, joking, drinking, buzzing around, they all seemed to have one eye on this conversation. Like they were awaiting some outcome.

"And for me," I said boldly, me and the champagne looking him squarely in the eyes.

"Certainly," Mr. Saltonstall said, brightly but without conviction. "Of course it's for you too."

"Good," I said. "Good. Now, tell me. How does it look? Have I got a chance to win, really?"

"Oh," he said, pulling back from me by a few very noticeable inches. "Oh, it looks quite good. Of the eight candidates for the preliminary runoff, four get into the final. I would be shocked if you did not reach the final."

"And then?"

"Then," he said, looking off over my shoulder. "Then. Well, Gordon, then, we just never know, do we? But if I were you, I would simply concentrate on having the best time of it I could have. This is a rare experience for a lad your age, a once-in-a-lifetime. Savor it. And do know, that all the people in this room are behind you ninety-nine percent."

Saltonstall stood up and started waving at somebody far across the room, the way you do when you want to get away from whoever you're with.

"Whoa," I said. "Isn't the saying *one hundred percent*? You know, 'We're behind you, old boy, one hundred percent.' Like that?"

He extended his hand and passed me a business card, smiling, grandfatherly. "If you need anything, Gordie. Just give us a call," he said, and slipped away.

I poured another glass of his champagne for myself and slouched there, staring at the card.

I n lieu of an entourage, or boosters, or hangers-on, or friends, like most political mucks haul around, I had Mosi. And with Sweaty Betty still awaiting her public apology, I had taken to picking Mosi up for school in the morning for the company, and because, if I couldn't at least show off the Tourismo for *somebody*, then what was it all for? However, this pretty well erased my last quiet, crisis-free portion of the day.

"You remember I told you I had a friend working on *The School Newspaper*?" he asked, offering me half of a savagely beaten banana. He looked like he was afraid I was going to do him likewise.

"Yup," I sighed, pulling away from his house. I heard the familiar opening chords of "Oh Jesus" in his voice.

"You want me to read it to you, or should we just wait till they tip the car over in the school lot?"

"Sing," I said.

" 'Responding to the results of last week's published poll, *alleged* candidate Gordon "Four Percent" Foley compared front-runner Robert O'Dowd to the transvestite played by Jaye Davidson in the film *The Crying Game*.' "

"Oh my *god*! No, Mosi, no. Please, tell me this is a joke. It doesn't say that."

Mosi paused. "Is that one of those things where you say 'Mosi, tell me blah blah blah,' because that's really what you want me to tell you, or because you wish it was the truth?"

"Oh my *god*!" I swerved the Tourismo through a red light, around stunned pedestrians, across the lane divider, before regaining control.

They could say what they wanted about my being out of touch, but I certainly understood the impact on one's lifespan of insulting a very popular member of the football team whose parents went away frequently and who threw reputedly excellent parties in their absence. Even if the team and the player actually sucked.

"There is more, if you're interested," Mosi added.

"What the hell. Once you're dead, you're dead, right? It's not like they can dig me up and kill me again."

"I don't know. I heard about these voodoo guys in New Orleans who—"

"Read, Mosi."

" 'Furthermore, Four Percent Foley had no idea that Marsha Brady, the fortyish former *Brady Bunch* character, was not, in fact, an Amber High student.' "

"God, what crap. If they called her Marsha Brady . . . of course I would have known. Who the hell knows who, ah . . ."

"Maureen McCormack."

"Right. Who the hell knows who she is, anyway? I guess now I know, huh, what the yellow frigging press does with the facts? Poor O.J.—you know, I almost believed he did it."

"Hey, Gordie, I was fooled too. But let me finish. Put both hands on the wheel now, okay?"

I did, carving small fingernail gouges into the wooden wheel. I leaned forward until my brow almost touched the windshield.

" 'In response to his dismal showing in the hearts of his fellow Amber High students, Four Percent Foley had this to say: "The question is, do I give a rat's ass? . . . Who, other than a complete putzball, would want to spend the greatest year of his life kissing asses to be elected head dildo of this peckerhead factory?" ' "

The horn sounded as I rammed my head into the center of the steering column. After a few seconds Mosi grabbed me by the hair and forced my eyes to the road just as I swerved toward an oncoming yellow school bus. With the two of us now steering, we guided the car to the curb, where, in a bold move, Mosi touched the gear shift for the first time ever. I did not protest as he parked us.

"I never talked to anybody from that ass-wipe toilet-paper rag of a—"

"You might want to think about choosing your words more carefully from here on," Mosi wisely cut in.

"But how . . . ?" I pleaded. "Who wrote the damn

thing?" I grabbed the paper out of his hands. Which freed him to finally peel the banana. " 'The *I-Team*'? Who the hell is the I-Team?"

"Investigative," he said, shrugging. "Seems they're doing a series. Undercover stuff. I guess they got spies on the team. One in our homeroom."

I draped the paper over my head like the pirate hats we used to make. I wished I was making pirate hats again. I really did.

"A series," I repeated, without inflection. "There is more to come. It's going to get worse."

He extended the remains of the banana again. Mosi seemed truly sad for me. "Sure you won't have some? I read that potassium is the stress mineral. Banana's got a shitload of potassium. For the stress, like."

I looked at Mosi's perfectly round face, still carrying the trace-tan of summer's end. And it came back to me, what it was I was after back when I was after something.

"*American Graffiti*, Mos. *Fast Times at Ridgemont High. Rock and Roll High School. Dazed and Confused.*"

God love him, Mosi tried to follow. "*National Velvet.*"

"Well . . . all right, in a way, *National Velvet.* My point is, it was supposed to be a different way, this senior-year moment. Not, like, something you wanted to do for the rest of your life, certainly, but I think we earned a right to a once-in-a-lifetime party here.

We've been looking forward to this for . . . years. And it's turning upside down, Mosi, getting away from me, way, way out of my control. And I'm afraid I'm just going to miss the whole goddamn thing, and that's going to be the end of it. Because you don't get invited into this situation again. I know it, you don't get a second crack at right now."

It wasn't that Mosi didn't already know everything I said, but I think it probably stings to hear somebody cry it out. And I don't think missing out on the party had ever occurred to him. He went far sadder than I'd ever seen him before, his laugh lines smoothing out to nothing so that he looked strange to me, like my mother would without her teeth.

"You'll get through it, Gordie," he said. "You'll have yours. This"—he waved his hands out the open window as if drying them in the breeze—"this'll stop after a while. Then you can play again."

The idea, spirit, the words themselves, lifted Mosi's mood as he said them. His face opened back up into the miraculous, convincing thing it was. I believed that face, and I got better.

"When does this edition come out?" I asked, laughing now as I aimed the Studebaker Gran Tourismo Hawk straight at the school, no weaving this time.

"Tomorrow," Mosi said, clapping me on the shoulder. "It's at the printer's now, and the school gets it before first bell in the morning."

"Well, good," I said. "At least I'll have one more day of relative peace before the shit parade."

I reached over, in my new light mood, and turned on the radio.

"If something good comes on, I'll peel out for you," I promised. Mosi clapped. "The Hawk is not just beautiful, you know. It can also fly."

Before the tubes warmed up and let the music out, the flip phone bleeped. It was like a little shot in my side, hunching me over. I turned off the radio before it could even sing. The phone bleeped again, and it scored again. I was just not going to be allowed off the ropes.

"I'll be there this afternoon, Da," I said as soon as I picked up.

"You'll be here *now*," he answered.

"I'm sorry, Gordie," Mosi said as I dropped him in front of school. "But I'm sure it'll get better soon. Hang in. You'll get to do all that *American Graffiti* stuff when it's over."

If you had walked in on my discussion that morning with my grandfather, you would not have been able to tell which of us was the prisoner and which was the free-range citizen. I never got up out of my chair as he paced and ranted and practically cried over what I was doing to the respected name he had spent decades of his life and millions of taxpayer dollars to

99

build. "Am I right here, Chuckie," he'd periodically ask the guard, "or am I wrong?" I thought Chuckie was going to hand his gun over to the old man.

I had heard there is a mental numbness that comes over a person who is stranded bobbing in a frigid ocean—which hadn't happened to me yet, but probably would—and that envelops a boxer who is taking a pounding but who cannot fall down. Something like that must have been happening to me when I heard Da out, waited for him to take a few puffs on his new portable oxygen apparatus, then stood to respond.

"When I find out who's been feeding you those stupid newspapers," I groaned, "I'm gonna scale him and gut him like a fish, wrap him in his own newspapers, and drop him face-up and mouth-open under the raw sewage drain over by the science museum."

Fins stopped sucking on air. The slits of his angry little red-veined eyes rounded and softened into them ol' smilin' eyes he sold for all those years. He turned, once again, to the guard.

"Do ya believe this, Chuckie? This late inta the game, and the kid suddenly develops some balls."

He liked it. Why couldn't my words ever achieve what my brain had planned?

"*That's* the killer drive you been lacking, Gordie. That's the thing I been waitin' ta see. A politician's gotta have that, or he's goin' nowhere."

"I hear nowhere's kind of nice this time of year."

"But the smart mouth," he said, waving the paper

at me, "that's gotta go. You go now, and take the attitude with you to the street, but don't say nothin' stupid no more."

I sat there, unsure whether I had been given any actual advice, instructions, or marching orders.

"Get up, go on, get out," he said, brooming me away with his long skeletal fingers, much more like a grandfather now than a godfather. "Next week is the primary runoff, Gordie, which you're going to place well in. Then is the school thing, which you're going to *win*, and then, on to the big pie."

"Which I'm going to—"

"Did you change the oil in the car?"

"Da—"

"Every two weeks, Gordie, whether you drive it or not. Change the oil every two weeks, like it's been getting for thirty years. The car'll know if you ain't doing it, and I'll know if you ain't doing it."

"Fine, Da," I said.

"And how 'bout money? You okay for money?" He reached into the pocket of his gray baggy prison pants and pulled out a wad.

"All set, Da," I said.

"Here, change the oil, and run it through a wash and wax."

Chuckie brought me the money, five twenties.

"Cloths, Gordie," Fins said into his oxygen mask. "Soft cloths, no frigging brushes. And don't forget to put the top up, for chrissake."

I drove straight to Jiffy Lube and made them let me stay in the car while it was up on the lift. It was nice up there, airborne and incommunicado for the entire fourteen minutes of the oil change. I had a thrilling view of a mountain of old radiators, batteries, rims, and tires humping up over the back of the auto-parts joint. It was all relaxing and simple and made sense, the way car parts do, and I was truly sorry when I found that Jiffy Lube's sub-fifteen-minute boast was no exaggeration.

The car wash I found—after driving past three places that used brushes—was worth the search. Jets jetted me from all sides as I squirmed around like a kid trying to catch it from every angle. The dream quality of it, the wild watery fantasy, was so complete that I wasn't even fully aware what I was fantasizing. And when we came out of the froth, the Studebaker Gran Tourismo Hawk whiter and shinier than it probably had been thirty years before, we were both new. We were both refurbished and reanimated and coated with two impenetrable sheets of Turtle Wax. We were ready.

There was so much Fins didn't know, about life for a guy like me. But he knew instinctively the power of a well-timed wash and hot wax.

When I finally showed up at school, well after lunchtime, I went to Vadala's office. It was becoming my center, since classroom activity was taking up less and less of my time.

"Okay, Mr. Vadala, what do you know about the I-Team?"

"Foley? Foley, could this be possible? You know, most people who cut actually stay out the whole day. It attracts less attention that way."

"I didn't cut, not really. I had to attend to some campaign-related business."

"Which campaign?"

"Both, actually. So it sort of counts as school time *and* Flex-Campus time, right?"

"I'll give you points for creativity, but no, it counts as cut time."

I shook my head, slid down into the chair many of us had slid down into before. "Oh, come on, Mr. Vadala. I could really use some indulgence here. I am a senior, you know."

"Yes, I know. And you're going to be one again next year if you don't pull it together."

I thought about that. Maybe, maybe. Another shot?

"Jesus, no. It could be even *worse* the second time around," I blurted.

"Yes, it could. So you'd better not miss any more days."

"Fine, Mr. Vadala. Now tell me, who are these

I-Team geeks who are out to get me?"

"I don't know. It's a secret." He got busy on his computer. The computer with all the in-depth files.

"Right. And if it's a secret, then *you* know about it. Everybody knows you're the dean of secrets."

Vadala looked up with a pleased little smile on his face. "Do they really say that?"

"They do indeed. So, who are my tormentors?"

"I can't tell you. This is their Flex-Campus assignment. They proposed to me an investigative-reporting project that required anonymity, and I have to respect that. Anyway, what would you do with the information?"

I hadn't even thought of that. "I'd . . . *reason* with them."

"Right," he said, dubious. "Or your grandfather'd liquidate them."

"Come on, Mr. Vadala. Have you heard the stuff they've been doing to me?"

"Well . . . I may have been privy to a little early information."

"So, then—"

"Did you say those things?"

"Well, no . . . not *officially*. Not on the *record*."

"Rule number one, Gordon: You are now a public figure. There is no such thing as off the record."

Of all the sad truths I'd had served up to me lately, this was the most deflating. Boy, I longed to get off the record.

"You're not going to help me out, are you, Mr. Vadala?"

"I cannot, Mr. Foley. Just watch yourself, that's all. That's all I can say to help you."

"Watch out now, babes in toyland!" Mad Matt was roaring, leaping, flailing, excited like he could not wait to get me on the air this time. "He's back, and more controversial than ever, and with a brand-new handle that just puts our Name the Candidate contest to shame. To *shame*. Here he is, Four Percent Foley!"

As Matt turned up the big-crowd-applause sound effect, and Sol laughed in my ear, I took the microphone. "What, does that school newspaper have a circulation of a *@#% million or something?"

"New game, constituents. As our young hero gets crustier and meaner as a result of the political hardball he's mixed up in, we're going to have to begin our censor-the-candidate watch. Four Percent is developing a salty speaking style."

"I'm sorry, Matt," I said on air. Which he seemed to appreciate. "And while I'm on the subject of apologizing, may I have a minute of your and your listeners' time to make something right?"

Sol sat there vigorously shaking his head no.

"Sol says no, Gordie." Matt grinned. "You got your minute. But keep it clean."

I took a long breath and, for the few seconds

before speaking, realized just how quiet and deep and lonely dead air really is.

"Last week on this program, I told somebody to shut up. Perhaps some of you heard that. Perhaps you laughed. Matt laughed, and Sol laughed. And since that came out of my mouth, things have been happening to me, things that haven't been any fun. It's a coincidence, of course, or maybe not, but the thing that's there and indisputable is that the bad things have been a lot worse because Betty has been apart from me. Not just like, she's over there and I'm over here, because we have that kind of separation lots of times and it doesn't hurt us. But, like, fractured. Because before, even when she wasn't there with me, she was right there, for me. And even though you probably couldn't tell from the outside, we had something, large, on the inside. And while I can sometimes call Sweaty a &\$!@* because she can be one and she'll tell you that herself, and even though she can call me . . . nevermind that . . . Anyway, what I cannot do is I cannot ever tell her to shut up, because I've got no right, and because no matter what she's saying, I'm an idiot to want her to stop.

"So, Betty, if you're listening, I hope this makes it as an apology because I've got no business telling you ever to shut up, ever, and in fact we'd all probably benefit from somebody telling me to. If you decide this is not apology enough, I will find out what is enough, and I will find a way to give it to you. I couldn't be sorrier and I couldn't be sadder, and I couldn't believe I could miss you like I miss you.

"And if you're not listening, we'll get you a tape."

After a great big fat uncomfortable pause, Matt came on and said, "Sure. I'm sure we can make her a tape." Then he went into joke mode, but just lightly. "And you went way over your one minute, Gord."

"I'm not making him any extra tapes," Sol muttered, ever the sport.

Off the air, I asked Matt, "Is it okay, Matt, if I call it a night?"

He nodded, waved me on out of the studio.

The call-in lights were all shining brightly as I passed them on the way out.

My ma was up, at the table again, when I got home. I stood in the doorway, could not manage to speak. I walked past her on the way to my room.

"I think maybe I will vote for you after all," she said, killing the kitchen light.

t was a better day. Though I expected a rash of shit when I got to school and faced the music over what was in *The School Newspaper*, I didn't fear it the way I feared it the day before. Betty was with me.

As I sat in the Studebaker, giving her her four minutes of warm-up, Sweaty Betty quietly slid in the passenger side.

"Accepted," she said, foofing her hair higher in the little square mirror on the sun visor. "You give good apology, Gordie. You should do it more often."

I took that without speaking, dropped the Hawk into gear, and tooled off to school feeling, unwisely, invulnerable.

We hadn't gotten out of the car, hadn't entered the parking lot even, before that new familiar feeling—like a bathtub drain whirlpool gurgling down from the center of my belly—rushed back. This was something so big that Betty at my side could not even match it.

"Holy shit." That was Sweaty Betty.

"Holy *shit*" was me.

Since we had the top down on this fine and heretofore carefree Indian summer morning, we had a clear view of it. The massive billboard, on top of the two-story sporting-goods store directly across from the front entrance of school, was a paid political advertisement.

On the other side of the street, spilling down from the top step and fanning out all over the block, was what appeared to be the entire student body.

My face on the billboard was the size of our garage door at home. In front of it, the Studebaker Gran Tourismo Hawk—being driven by a smiling, waving *Fins* Foley, circa 1973, with big long sideburns and a shirt collar that could have made it as a skateboard ramp. They looked to be pulling into the big empty garage of my head.

On the one side, that, the billboard. On the other side, them, the student body.

That.

Them.

Then there was me. Live and in person, driving the famous vehicle right through the middle of it.

You would have thought the Hawk burned nitrous oxide, the way Sweaty Betty began—and could not stop—laughing at me when the crowd started screaming, "Four-Per-Cent! Four-Per-Cent!"

"Goddammit, Fins," I said. "What are you doing to me?"

The phone rang.

"Go to hell, you senile old crock!" I yelled, and felt much better. The phone, however, went on ringing. I went on not answering it.

I scrambled, one hand on the wheel, one hand on

the toggle switch to get the top up and stop the rain of ridicule from beating down on me. "If you don't *mind*," I interrupted Sweaty's laugh-out, "could you please roll up that window?"

She did, but once the car was sealed up it only made the noise coming from my girl, my strength, my support, sound more brutal.

"Glad to have you back, Sweat," I said as I jumped on the gas with both feet and blasted right on past school.

"Glad to be back," she answered, leaning her head on my shoulder and squeezing me tight, as if we were on a roller coaster together.

By the time we actually did slink into school, homeroom and first period were gone. Betty patted me on the ass like a coach and said good luck as she shoved me toward biology.

Inside the door, the first thing that struck me was Mosi's face.

I had forgotten to pick him up that morning. Because I had Betty back.

I was only vaguely aware of the low laughter, the good-natured pokes in the ribs, the remarks, as I crossed the room toward my friend's desk. "I'm sorry, Mos. I'm such an asshole."

"Good thing you're so good at apologizing," he said. "I take it Betty is back."

"There's just no excuse. I can't tell you—"

Mosi held out his hands. "So don't tell me. Just don't forget me no more. Right now you got bigger problems than me anyway." He pointed over toward my desk. That is, he pointed over to the desk behind my desk. Where Robert O'Dowd was sitting cracking his knuckles, biting a loose piece off his pinky fingernail, then cracking his knuckles some more.

"He's not even *in* this damn class," I whined.

"No? You know, I didn't think so either," Mosi said. "But there he is, so apparently he is."

"If Four Percent Foley will ascend to his throne," Mr. San Pedro yukked, "we can commence."

"When you're school superintendent, Mosi . . ." I said, pointing out San Pedro for a hit.

I could feel O'Dowd's breath on my neck. Bastard, he wouldn't just smack me, wouldn't say anything. He simply hung back there, leaning closer, closer on me, breathing so I could feel the hot mist of his meanness gathering on my skin. Completely disorienting me and leaving me unable to recognize the words as the teacher spoke them.

The phone bleep-bleeped, my whole head heated to about 115 degrees with embarrassment, and I answered. Not before everyone turned to look at me, of course.

"D'ya *love* it? D'ya *love* it?" Fins boomed.

I could not answer immediately, as Mr. San Pedro was now standing, smiling, rocking on his feet right beside me.

"Is this something you'd like to share with the rest of us?" he asked, updating an old classic.

"Da, not now," I snapped into the phone.

"Duh. Then when?" San Pedro asked, to big laughs.

There is nobody more bloodthirsty than a teacher getting laughs. He looked all around, lapping it up. In the rush, he snagged the phone out of my hand.

"Um, sweetie, could His Honor please call you back? See, he's in the middle of high school right now."

Everybody laughed. San Pedro laughed. But only for an instant. You could see his face drain as Fins apparently started speaking, and San Pedro started listening. And nodding.

"It's a phone, Teach," somebody called out. "He can't hear you nodding."

Pale and trembling, the teacher handed me back the flip phone.

"San Pedro," I said loudly into the phone, even though Da hadn't asked. "San, capital P . . ." I raised my hand, just like I was a normal student, which, unfortunately, I'd never be again. "Mr. San Pedro, okay if I take this out in the hall? Thanks."

I could feel a bit of a shift as I strolled out with the phone on my ear. I was once again borrowing it from my grandfather, but some version of power was definitely clinging to me—much to my surprise.

Out in the hallway, things got back to normal.

"No, Da, I'm not thrilled. This does not help me. How is it going to look, a guy taking a serious run at the mayor's job, when he gets himself wedgied in the damn bathroom every day. 'Cause that's what they do to guys here, Da. They wedgie them."

"For what? You're a big man there now. They gotta see that."

"What they see is that I'm sitting on your knee while you have your hand stuck up my ass wiggling your fingers to make me talk. So now I'm going to show up at my next Chamber of Commerce breakfast with my underwear yanked up out of my pants, pulled over the back of my head, and strapped off under my chin."

Da, being from a different era, and of a very different political-social philosophy from me, heard a different urgency in my words than what I'd intended.

"So," he said coolly, "who exactly is going to do this to my grandson?"

"Oh Jesus, Da, it doesn't matter. Want to know what matters? It's that I'm a *senior*. Seniors aren't supposed to get wedgies. This is all backward."

"It's the guy, that sweet-boy from the newspaper article, isn't it? The one you said stuff about, right? What was his name?"

I thought about O'Dowd sitting back there waiting for me, breathing for me.

"I don't know, Da. I don't know what you're talking about. Let's just drop it."

"Fine. I'll get his name outta the paper."

Somehow, in there somewhere, I felt a threat toward *me*. Not like a physical threat. Something foggier.

"So," Fins said after a pause. "You don't like my present?"

"No," I said, the first time I could recall telling the truth when I knew he didn't want to hear it. Probably the first time anyone—outside of the law-enforcement community—had done so in decades.

The fiddling he did then with the phone, the heavy breathing into his apparatus, made me shudder at the blast that was coming. He didn't take stuff so beautifully well as a rule, and he would wind himself up before blasting me.

"I'm sorry," he said weakly. "I meant ta do something good for you. Thought you'd be happy." He hung up.

I felt like a rat.

As I retook my seat, O'Dowd practically climbed over his desk to haunt me now.

"You ain't foolin' nobody," he said. "We all know what you are."

"You do? Jeez, be a sport and let me in on it, because I haven't got a *clue* what I am at this point."

O'Dowd clapped me a sharp smack, right across the back of my head. Nobody in an official capacity, like, say, a teacher, seemed to notice. This was when I realized, the joke of all this was pretty much over.

Which always had the unfortunate effect of making me joke more.

"You shouldn't bite your fingernails, O'Dowd, or a hand will grow in your stomach. Didn't your mother ever—"

"You're going to be sorry you ever heard the name Robert O'Dowd," he interrupted.

"Well, actually, I already am," I said. "So I guess there's no need to continue, huh?"

He smacked me again. It was upon me now. Was I just going to let him beat my ass? Or was I going to put up an honorable defense before he beat my ass? I truly didn't know.

Good thing a miracle came along.

"Cut the crap, O'Dowd." It was the voice of an angel. Her name was Mariah Maris.

"Ya, O'Dowd, damn ape. Leave him alone," Tyra Mays joined.

I could feel O'Dowd back off, lean away from me, even as he said, "Shut yer faces." O'Dowd had dated them both at some point, and he was the type of ladies' man–psychopath who didn't like to let one job cross over the other. If girls frowned on his bullying, he wouldn't do it—not in front of them, anyway.

Neither of the girls had ever paid me much attention before, so this did come as a surprise. Anyway, I was happy to have their pity, and nodded my deep gratitude.

Tyra leaned across the aisle, put a hand lightly on

my wrist. "I heard you on the radio last night," she whispered. "That was so sweet . . . I cried."

Hmmm . . .

"I do wish you hadn't gone home so soon the other night," Matt said. "It was unbelievable. Half the women in the city must have called to say how sweet you were. Since you were gone, I had to absorb all the love in your stead."

"You're a trooper, Matt."

"Don't I know it. But hey, no joke. We're on to something here. You suddenly look viable. Not like you have a chance to win or anything, but, like, you *exist* anyway."

"What, because I apologized to my girlfriend?" I still wasn't sure if Mad Matt was suckering me.

He shrugged. "Go figure. I suppose maybe it's possible that men, y'know, in general, aren't prone to talking to their gals the way you talked to yours on the air. *I* don't happen to believe that, but our callers seemed to find you a phenomenon." He shrugged again.

I shrugged in return. Sol registered no reaction.

"Anyhow, kid," Matt said as he backed toward his spot for the start of the show. "You keep it up. You're an original. We love ya." He blew me a kiss, and signed on.

"Hell-oooo, ladies and gentlemen and ladies. It's

showtime again, and he's baaaaack. Mister Sensitive. Mister Wonderful. Mister Ladykiller. Missssster I'm-so-sorry. That's right, start those hearts a-throbbin' for Gordon 'Four Percent' Foley!"

I sat dumbstruck listening to the intro. Why did he always sound so supportive talking to me in person, when ten seconds later on the public airwaves I wound up sounding like a simp?

That's showbiz, I figured.

Matt was pointing at me repeatedly to join in. Sol slapped my arm, grabbed the mike, and practically shoved it in my mouth.

"Hi," I said.

"There you go, folks. Sensitive, yes, but also strong and silent. I hate to belabor the demigod thing, but . . . anyhow, he's here now and we're not letting him go this time. Girls, give the boy a call. You don't even have to ask your parents because we're *not*—not yet, anyway—a 900 number. And as for you guys out there, well, sit back and shut up. Gordie's a real man and doesn't need you anyway."

It was audible over the air when I let my head drop and smash into the microphone.

"Oh, that remark wouldn't seem to help the campaign," Sol deadpanned. "Is that kind of thing helpful, Four?" As we were getting to be really close now, Sol shortened my name to Four.

The calls, though, against all odds, turned out to be a boost.

"Oh, um, like, Gordie, ah, Mr. Foley, I just wanted to say that it took a real man to talk like you did to that Sweaty person like you did in front of so many ears. My boyfriend said you were a wuss, but he's a loser anyway."

"Gordie." This voice was deeper and sultry, probably ten years older than the previous caller. Maybe even voting age. "I just want to tell you that I don't care what other speeches I hear in this campaign, you've won my vote. And are you going to be out on any baby-kissing tours before the election?"

Sol cued up a woo-woo sound effect, then Mad Matt cut in. "He'll be touring the clubs on Landsdowne Street about midnight on Saturday, babe. Wear a pink corsage and something strapless."

Everybody was so much faster than me.

"Ah, I love babies," I said.

Matt cut off his mike. "Shut up," he yelled at me.

"Yes, hi, Gordie? One quick question: My boyfriend Pauly, right? He wants to have sex with me. And, well, I say, Okay, but you have to tell me you love me first. Right, so he says, Ya, sure, you know I do. So I say, Great, then tell me. So he does it again, he says, Of course, you know I do. So I say it again, Good, Pauly, so tell me. And he says it again, You know I do. So the thing is, does that count? Even though he can't actually, you know, *say* it? I think maybe it does, huh? He really loves me, right, Gordie? Technically, does the you-know-I-do stuff qualify, and if so, should I go ahead and sleep with him?"

Matt cut in before I could even close my fell-open mouth.

"I love you, I love you, I love you, I love you."

"Thanks," she said.

Dead air.

"Seems to me," I finally croaked, "that if a guy can't say a word, there should be some sort of rule that he can't perform it either."

Dead air.

"So . . . I should, then?" she said uncertainly.

I sighed, tiring too quickly these days. "Ya, sure, go ahead," I said.

She thanked me with a squeal and a giggle, and Pauly hollered, "Thanks, dude," laughing in the background. The phone slammed down before I could get back to her to fix what I'd done.

But not before I felt the stinging in my belly for it.

"Hello? This is Maureen Tisdale-Morrissey calling."

Matt swung for the fences. "Mau-reeeen Tis-dale-Mor-ris-sey!" He signaled Sol, who instantly hit up the theme music from Dragnet: Buuuuum de bum bum.

"Maureen Tisdale-Morrissey. The esteemed deputy mayor, former very close associate of one Fins Foley, and, most importantly, current front-runner in the mayoral runoff election. See, Gordie, it's official, there isn't a woman left who can resist you. Maureen, tell us, are you going to vote for our boy?"

All I could think of: Set up. Again. I was set up. Again.

"Well, Matt, I have to be honest and say that no, I don't believe I will. I think I'm still going to go with me."

"Well then, must be a clandestine rendezvous with the candidate you're sniffing around for. That's the other reason the ladies are all calling."

She laughed. "Well, Matt, don't think it hasn't crossed my mind. I'm only human."

I stopped thinking about the setup. I started listening to her. They talked about me, in front of me, as if I weren't even there. Like adults had always done when I was a kid.

"Actually," Maureen continued, "my daughter would be more interested in Mr. Foley. She told me to say hi to him."

I was confused. Was the opposition being nice to me? I had been told not to expect that. Or was she zinging me and I just didn't get it?

"How old's your daughter?" Matt tossed.

"Eleven," she returned.

Zing.

"Seriously, though," Maureen added, "I wanted to call and say that I think it's a fine thing Gordie is doing here. I believe the young people should be very involved in the political process, as a learning experience at least. He's a fine boy, and has been since the first time I met him, which was, I believe, when he was batboy at one of his grandfather's legendary soft-ball barbecues."

I had forgotten all about that. She made me all waxy for a minute there, thinking about this whole political-dynasty thing the way I used to think of it—as softball and Italian ice and love spilling all over my grandfather for no particular reason.

"I remember," I interrupted politely. "That was fun."

"Yes it was, Gordie," she said sweetly. "We all had a lot of fun over the years. I was glad to be a part of it. And, to let you in on a little secret, if I were not running myself, I probably would vote for you for mayor."

"Whoa," Matt said. "If that's not the most ringing nonendorsement I've ever heard . . . Listen, Maureen—can I call you Mo?"

"Absolutely not."

"Okay, Maureen, when can we get you down here, face-to-face with young Foley, on the show? It'll be dynamite."

"No, no," she said. "I'm not going for any of that. In fact, if my campaign manager knew I was on the air this long, he'd have a fit. I only called out of my personal fondness for Gordie, and out of respect for his family. What I would like to do though—Gordie, are you still there?"

"Oh, ah, ya."

"What I would like is to get together with you personally, off the air. To have a friendly discussion of issues just between us."

I shuddered. She was a professional, and had her sights on me now, knowing me to be a fake. This was the same feeling O'Dowd gave me.

Except she was so *nice*.

"Okay," I said. "You wanna come to my house?"

Maureen laughed. "You're cute. No, I think a power breakfast at the Meridien will do. One day next week—after the primary."

"After?" Matt asked, sounding much more astounded than he needed to, I thought. "What if— god forbid—our boy is no longer in the race after Tuesday?"

Maureen smiled. You know how you can hear that sometimes over the phone, when a person smiles? She smiled a big generous one. "Gordie will be in the final. He *will* make it through the primary. That's a prediction."

"Holy smokes, a bona fide prediction, right here on my show," Matt gushed. "That's never happened before. At least, not a *correct* prediction anyway."

"Thank you," I said to Maureen, as if she had actually somehow placed me into the final. "And, ya, breakfast. It's a date."

"My people will call your people," she said. "Bye-bye."

"My people get home from work at about six," I said.

Matt cued up a song and started playing it low, under the chatter. "We Are the Champions," by

Queen. A bit optimistic, I thought, but it gave me a little rush anyhow.

"Wow. She was really, really nice," I said, on air, about my main opposition.

It occurred to me that I probably shouldn't have done that. But Matt cranked the song, and I didn't care what I shouldn't have done.

As primary day approached, things got hot. I registered. Not to vote, which I had forgotten to do before the deadline and which would have proven embarrassing to the campaign had Da not informed me that of course I was registered—retroactively.

No, I *registered*. I was on the map, all over it, in fact. Small news items started appearing here and there, from press releases my diligent campaign workers produced.

"Foley vows to raise pay for all city teachers."

"Did I say that?" I asked Bucky, who was communicating with me more over the FinsFone, less and less face-to-face.

"Yes, you did, you populist hero. And let me compliment you on a masterstroke. That kind of thing plays *big*. Keep it up and soon you'll be as beloved as you-know-who."

"Thanks. Second question: Can I do that? Raise their salaries?"

"Not a chance."

"So why did I—"

"Listen, take a day out of the office today. Go

shoot some hoops down at the Boys' Club."

This too was becoming a familiar pattern. I was almost never required at the office anymore. Which was fine, since the office was a serious drag, with the snotty college kids figuring me out, bossing me around, using words they knew I couldn't understand.

"Fine with me," I said. If I was going to spend my Flexible Campus days working on my J, that would be fine with me. Then, when my fairy-tale stint as boy mayor and hot radio ga-ga deejay was over, I'd hit the NBA running. Could happen.

I'd probably shot hoops at the Boys' Club a thousand times before. Sometimes with Mosi. Sometimes with Sweaty. Sometimes with a few of the last-cut school b-ball rejects who were just about my speed. And lots of times, since it wasn't really a very popular club, by myself. Which, of course, is the best way to shoot hoops, because you can be great, when you're alone in a gym.

But I had never shot with actual Boys' Club members before. Certainly not perfect fund-raiser-commercial, dirty, happy needy ragamuffins from a Dickens Boys' Club. Yet in they tramped, boisterous and happy and annoying as hell, breaking the great silence, stealing the ball from me, taunting me.

The photographer—but of course—came in just in time to catch me looking like a dolt, chasing after squealing gargoyles a foot shorter than me who simply refused to give me back my ball.

"Foley Pledges Complete Support to Struggling Inner - City Program."

That was the headline over the photo op. The caption read, "Mayoral candidate Gordon Foley has a ball with city kids."

They always had a place for me to go. Something's being built, Gordie. Run over there and get your picture taken at the groundbreaking. Something's being torn down, Gordie. Get over there and look forlorn. But remember, don't *say* anything, for chrissake. We'll release a statement lamenting the passing of an era.

An extended interview with me was printed in *The South Side Sentinel*, a weekly tabloid that was a longtime Fins Foley mouthpiece. I must admit, I came off very witty and sincere and informed on all the issues. I talked about my girlfriend, making her sound like Sweet Polly Purebred, and my mom, making her sound . . . actually, making her sound just like she is. I got misty over the whole thing. I hope to someday meet the man who allegedly interviewed me, so I can thank him.

My junior-year yearbook picture accompanied the article.

I started getting letters. From girls. Too young to vote, mostly, or too old for . . . anything.

School was a different story. Another issue of *The School Newspaper* was out—sigh—and I sat in the library reading it. Mosi no longer delivered me the bad news, unable to bear it, I supposed, so I had to pick it up in the street or the library like everyone else.

"... began his speech to supporters with the questionable joke ... 'What's on the plate, cocaine?' "

"I can't believe it. I cannot believe these no-life I-Team ginks sent somebody to my fund-raiser."

I read on.

"It turned out to be only a taste, a sampling of what appears to be a pattern of drug references that the candidate cannot resist making, such as this from his candidate questionnaire profile ..."

I threw the paper across the library, pages spreading out and fluttering to the floor like autumn leaves.

Smack. I was clomped across the back of the head.

"I'll pick it up," I said, figuring it was Mrs. Clancy, the hundred-and-twelve-year-old bantam librarian.

"I don't give a shit if you pick it up." It was O'Dowd. He smacked me again.

"I wish you'd stop *doing* that," I snapped.

"Oh, do you really?" he answered.

Smack. I didn't feel that one, only heard it. It was Mrs. Clancy. She smacked O'Dowd.

"Leave him alone, ya punk," she said.

O'Dowd raised a backhand as if to whack Mrs. Clancy with it. Just for show. Even O'Dowd wouldn't hit Mrs. Clancy.

"Oh, I just wish you'd try it, ya punk. Ya coward."

If I had one tenth of her spit ... I thought.

"I read your interview in the *Sentinel*," she said, smiling at me. "You sounded very nice. Good boys talk about their mothers like that."

"Oh, ya?" said O'Dowd. "Have you read *The School Newspaper*?"

"No!" she barked. Then she shushed him. "No talking in my library. And don't you lay another finger on this boy."

The bell rang, and my study period ended. O'Dowd, who didn't actually have a study period, followed me out, toward the next class he wasn't supposed to be in with me. Once in the hallway, with hundreds of students crisscrossing, he stepped on the heel of my shoe, giving me a flat tire. When I bent over to fix it, he stepped up behind me, kneed me hard in the tailbone, and sent me crashing down on my face.

Traffic in the hallway, in the immediate area around where I'd sprawled, stopped. I recognized all the faces that stared down at me, but I didn't really *know* anybody. Because for so long I was happy enough to have it that way. Most of the faces showed some kind of pity, but they weren't exactly giving it up to me. O'Dowd, of course, was leering down at me, then around at the spectators for approval, then down at me again.

It came over me then that I needed to say something. That I needed to address my peers. From right there flat on the floor.

"I never wanted this, you know. I never really wanted any of this stuff that's going on here. It just all kind of was dumped on me, and then things got out of my control, and then words started coming out . . . that really had nothing to do with me. With who I really am."

I didn't know what I was trying to accomplish there, but—maybe because I spoke to them from the seat of my pants—I seemed to make contact with my classmates. Probably for the first time.

Burt Sybertz, a behemoth of a football lineman and a shot-putter, a useful athlete but with zero star quality, put his hand out to me. "You don't have to be a dick *all* the time, Bob," he said to O'Dowd.

As I took Burt's hand and he pulled me up nearly off my feet, I repeated, "Well, like I said, I never really wanted this in the first place." When I was standing, I was face-to-face with O'Dowd.

"But I want it now," I said.

showed up at my local polling station shortly after it opened at seven A.M. It was in the basement of the Curley School, which I had attended from kindergarten through sixth grade. Not all that long ago, as one of my old teachers pointed out on her way in to vote. I reminded her to remember me when she pulled that lever. She patted me on the head.

I wore a blue jacket with gold buttons, a powder-blue shirt with a white collar, and a painted Jerry Garcia tie from Bloomingdale's. I never thought I could feel good in a jacket and tie, but I felt real good. My dad had bought me the outfit as a primary-day present, giving it to me at breakfast that morning.

"So," I said. "I've won you over. You're in my corner."

"Son, I am always in your corner. I have been so pleased to see you taking on new challenges, reaching for something, working. I'm really proud of you, Gordie . . ."

My father is a very precise speaker. When he talks, you can hear the commas, you can hear the question marks and the semicolons. And you can hear the ellipses.

"But . . ." I helped him along.

"But, I never voted for my father, and I'm not voting for you. I love you both, but I don't love your version of public service."

"Jeez, Dad. Y'know? This is a hairy day for me. You *could* fake it. You could just lie. It's a secret ballot, not like I could check on you."

"Gordie . . . I considered that. Then I reconsidered. I figure, when the smoke clears, I will have done more for you, as your father, by showing you what I value and standing behind it." He shook his head at himself, working it out as he spoke it. "Does that make any sense to you?"

"Well, my head's kind of busy today. But, ya, it makes a little. And I have a feeling—when the smoke clears—it'll make more."

He smiled. As far as he was concerned, I got it. And for the moment, that was good enough for both of us. I smiled back.

"Anyway," Dad said, knotting my new tie around his own neck because he knew I had no idea how the thing worked. "I wanted to make sure you looked fine on your day." He slipped the tie up over his head and lowered it over mine, even though I only had on a T-shirt yet. "I hope you win without me, Gordie."

"Actually, Dad, I was sort of hoping I could lose *with* you."

So I went out into the fray with the feeling I could not lose. Just a feeling, a funny, unrealistic thing a guy's dad can give him without hardly trying.

Fins had called me, and Bucky had called me, but that was all pep talk and bluster. This was a workday for me, and no press release from my staff could pretend to be me. I hit the booth, voted for myself—the first time I had voted for anyone—and stepped back out into the light with a strange feeling, a powerful feeling.

Not that I had voted for me. But that I had *voted*. I really *was* a player now.

"Remember Gordon Foley when you cast your ballot."

"Hi, I'm Gordon Foley. Think of me when you're voting."

"Gordon Foley for mayor. Thank you."

"Fordon Goley. I'm your man."

"Hi. Uh . . . bye."

"Hi, ma'am, Gordon Foley here. Can I kiss your baby?"

"Well, yes, he is my grandfather."

"It's parked right over there across the street. Sure you can look at it, right after you go in there and vote for me."

I handed out my flier to everybody with hands. If they raised those hands to refuse, I pretended not to understand, and slipped it between their fingers. Six feet farther down the sidewalk lay a small carpet of my literature, with the black-and-white picture of me grinning and waving as I stood up in the Studebaker Gran Tourismo Hawk.

"Will you please consider me when you're making your choice for mayor?"

It had become almost mindless. The words had begun to float from my lips without being launched by me. Until somebody heard, and responded.

"Yes," the woman said, "I will consider you. But will *you* consider *me*?"

Whoa. It hadn't occurred to me that these would be two-way conversations.

"Sure," I said. I shrugged.

"All right. What I need is some day care that doesn't cost more than what I make on the job I need the day care for."

It wasn't like she was asking for a new convention center downtown. I figured this must be in that big old hundred-million-dollar budget easy. "I guarantee it," I said, shaking her hand. Hey, nobody said I couldn't.

She smiled. Warmly. Maybe incredulously, but warmly. She didn't believe me. I scribbled the FinsFone number on one of my fliers and handed it to her.

"If I haven't done anything about this within three months, you call me direct."

The smile turned to a giggle and a shake of the head. I didn't know what she was laughing about; *I* was dead serious.

But it sure felt good anyhow.

Can-do. I can, and I did. I made that lady smile, and it was a breeze.

I did it again as soon as I could.

"Of course, there's got to be some way to get you that check sooner than six months later," I huffed. "*That*'ll be fixed."

"Just like the old man would do," the old guy praised.

"Nobody's going to tell you you can't put a satellite dish in your own backyard, not as long as I'm on the beat."

It looked, and felt, so different up close. I could do things. I could merely speak, and worlds improved. I wasn't sure I wasn't lying, but I actually felt like I could fix everything. What a rush.

I wanted to win now.

Except I didn't want the *job*. I wanted to win the election, without being stuck being mayor.

It got pretty old pretty fast, though. Asking for votes, smiling all the time, talking to people . . . The highlight of the day came when Mosi and Betty and several of her friends came by to help work the polls for an hour.

"Maybe I can give the fliers out to people," Mosi said, surprising me. It was a strange version of Mosi talking to me, distant, kind of sad.

I handed him the fliers. "Knock 'em dead, killer," I said, and watched him assault the voters. I smiled—

the real one, not the candidate one—as I watched him awkwardly work the crowd. I saw people do a double take as they realized Mosi, with his thick, dark features, big head, big hair, big arms and shoulders, and glassy eyes, was trying to give them something rather than take something away from them. It was obvious between my man Mosi, affirming many people's fears about letting teenagers into the power industry, and Betty's Boop Troops charming the male vote but chilling the female, that I was losing more support than I was gaining.

While I did not want to lose the primary, this setback was the most enjoyable part of the show so far.

"Can't you stay with me awhile?" I asked Sweaty as the Foley contingent began folding up camp.

"Stuff to do, Mr. Mayor," she answered. "Frankly, we love our man to pieces, but we're going to have to be with you mostly in spirit, 'cause this shit is, like, dullest."

I nodded, and wished I could go with her.

"Thank you," I said.

"Don't thank me now. Tonight. When they have some meaningful numbers, you come pick me up, and we'll have a little celebrate."

The candidate was infused with sudden renewed vigor.

"Ya?"

"Ya. I'll be home, hot dog."

Sweaty and her friends took off, to get back to life,

to real life, to high school and boy-tease and pizza life that was their right and that I was piss-eyed jealous over. I stared at the last of them piling onto the bus, and kept staring as the bus pulled out, passed directly in front of the polling station, and somebody mooned me.

I sighed. I got a pang of lonely. I used to like lonely.

For a few minutes I stopped campaigning. I leafed through other people's literature. I found out that sheriff isn't nearly the cool gig it sounds like, running desperadoes out of town; in reality it's more like he baby-sits the jail. I also found that it requires no skill or background of any kind to qualify as a state senator. Maybe I was just after the wrong job.

Then I stopped reading, and I watched them work.

They all looked like asses.

The voters, who in a few hours would move some of these same people a step closer to positions of power, were treating the candidates as if they were panhandlers with dead fish in their pockets. And the candidates behaved as if they appreciated it.

I fell back against the yellow-brick wall of the Curley School. "What the hell are we doing?" I asked the candidate for state senate, Michael Morris.

"We're kissing the public butt."

"Okay," I said. "So why?"

"Because during the day I usually work in my aunt's dry cleaner. I don't want to do that. I don't want people telling me, 'Hey, you didn't get the sweat stain out from the underarm of my shirt,' anymore. I want people asking me for favors. I want to be head of a committee that tells a developer, 'No, you can't build your restaurant there, because *I* said so,' and I want to be the guy who tells the Indians, 'Enough already with your damn casinos.' I want to be that guy. I want to make a noise, y'know?"

I thought about it. I knew what he was talking about, but honestly, I couldn't work it up like he could.

"And help people, you mean?"

"Ya . . . that's part of it, of course, but . . . you know what I'm talking about." He slapped me backhanded across the shoulder. "You're in the business. You're practically a power broker already."

That was it, the thought that finally made me feel stupider than anything.

Power broker. This was what my da had given his adult life to. Not the *what* of what you could do with power, but the having of it for its own sake.

Back at my groveling station. The work was hard, harder than anything I'd done in the campaign so far, and I got sweaty marching up and down the street, shaking hands and smiling and being nicer than I felt like being after a while. Around eleven o'clock Fins had called to check on things, and I rushed him, telling him things were great but that I had to get back to my post. He was giggly. My grandfather was not a giggly man, not even in victory. His first acceptance speech, all those years ago, was famous for having to be bleeped over while Fins wailed away at his beaten foe.

He called again at eleven thirty and twelve thirty and two, but I stopped answering.

By then I wanted to go home. I wasn't consumed by the outcome of this right now. I didn't especially care if they made me mayor or pope or god right there by popular demand; I just didn't want to be there. Many, many—mostly old—well-intentioned people came by to tell me how much they loved my da, to relate wonderful tales of how he had mangled the law to do something chivalrous for this struggling family or that. One grand-looking little dame—there was no other way to look at her—in a pink sombrero-size hat tried her damnedest to tell me a very personal story of herself and my grandfather one evening in the Tourismo—*my* Tourismo—which made the little hairs on my arms prickle and which I was *not* going to listen to.

"*That* car," she said, pointing shamelessly at the Studebaker across the street. "That fresh, brassy little—"

"It's not the same car," I interrupted. "This one's a fake. One of those copies they make from a kit. The real one he drove off the bridge in Narragansett."

The old woman deflated. I thought it was because of the car, and I felt bad.

"I thought Narragansett was *our* spot," she moaned. She left me without another word, but with a very Maureen-for-mayor look on her face.

It didn't matter anymore what people said to me, if they were going to vote for me, if they loved Fins and were 'sure the cub was gonna be just like the old lion,' wink wink. I had, halfway through the day, learned possibly the biggest life-lesson I was going to learn from the whole political experiment:

There is nothing harder than pretending to care about what you're doing, when you're really not convinced you do.

Do all of us politicians run out of gas this quickly?

It was starting to show, as fewer and fewer people came up to me.

"I'll hang around with you if you want."

It was Mosi. I hadn't even realized he hadn't gotten on the bus with the rest of them earlier.

"Hey," I said, excited. "You're here."

"Hey," he answered. "I am. Got any more fliers? I gave all mine out already."

I put my hand on his shoulder. "I'm so glad you stayed, Mos."

"Ya? Well, good. Do you feed your volunteers? I'm starvin', like."

I laughed and laughed, more than he thought made sense.

"Pretty easy to amuse these days, Gordie. Ain't getting many laughs lately, huh?"

I stopped laughing, shook my head no.

"I'm sorry for that," Mosi said. Then he shrugged, because what else could he do? "Got any fliers?" he repeated. "Got any food?"

I looked at his round face, and it brightened my spirits. But it didn't give me any more energy for going back to the job I didn't want to do.

"No, and no," I said. "Let's go eat."

Mosi beamed. "You're the man."

"Remember, Mr. Mayor, don't inhale now."

I laughed, choked, laughed. Choked.

"He's in the inhaling, the devil is. Can't let him get in you, that devil. Long as you don't inhale, the devil stays out of your deepest, most secret, most important parts. You can still be a virgin the other way."

I picked up the guitar and played. Jesus, I was good. My god, I was good. I was loud and I was fast and I was really, really good. *Brilliant* would not be too strong a word.

Mosi has a microwave in his private padded garage with the many guitars and the TV and the stereo. Mosi's parents buy him whatever toys he wants and give him his privacy in his padded-garage world, just as long as he promises not to get a driver's license because they don't want him behind the wheel of a car. That's the deal.

Mosi's parents love him.

So do I.

So Mosi had the microwave and the Foley campaign sprung for every single frozen burrito they had at the Li'l Peach.

Mosi was plucking a wine-sweet tune out of his orange sunburst Fender Telecaster when me and my lead belly fell asleep on the hard carpeted floor of the soft padded garage.

I was still a little fuzzy as I sat with my parents watching the day's events play out on the TV. (I think it was the burritos hanging with me longer than anything else.)

I couldn't believe it was me up there.

"I'll tell you what, Gordie," my father joked. "If you *don't* finish at least fourth in *this* field, I'm changing my name."

He was right. With this being a special runoff election for my grandfather's suddenly vacated job, there wasn't the usual time to thin out the field of crackpots, so the race was open to anybody who could get the three hundred signatures and find the office to file. Fringers. Libertarians who wanted to gain control of the government so they could then disband it. One-note wackos like the antidog guy, the antirecycling guy, the pro–assault-rifle lady. It seemed like every concerned citizen, every community activist who ever saved a tree and got his picture in the paper, and every part-time real-estate broker with too much free time was in the contest, threatening to wake this town up and put it right after decades of "old-school political hackdom and machine dictatorship."

Nobody mentioned any names, but we in the Foley household all shifted in our seats every time we heard the reference.

I could not believe it was me. Like a cloud of smoke and thirty feet of space separated me from my image on the screen. It didn't look like me, didn't move like me. The people who greeted that me did not treat him the way real people ever treated me.

Unfortunately, the haze lifted fairly early for me. The haze of the afternoon, and the haze of feeling like the election was there, in my TV, and I was here, in my family home.

Maureen Tisdale-Morrissey laid a beating on everybody. A brutal beating. The other candidates combined did not add up to her percentage.

The number two candidate was the chief of police, a man nearing retirement who already had a good job and a good pension to look forward to.

Number three was a personal-injury lawyer who was famous as the first guy in the country to advertise for clients in a big way on TV. He was so rich from marketing his ad-strategy video to other lawyers that he pledged to take no salary if elected.

Number four, a fraction behind number three, but way, way, way ahead of the rest of the pack, was a local high-school student and radio personality who drove a nice car and dated the most excellent girl since the beginning of girls.

"I knew you could do it," my mother said as the newscaster declared the top four slots locked up two hours before the polls closed. She leaned over and kissed me on the head. "I think it was my vote that put you over."

"Sorry, babe," Dad said as he stood to shake my hand. "I canceled you out."

"I hate it when you do that," she said as the phone rang.

"It's got to be for you," Dad said, laughing a sadistic little laugh. "You might as well just camp out with the phone now. Your life is over."

"Ma," I whined, "do I have to get that?"

Ma picked it up, said some warm greetings, some thank-yous, some nice-to-hear-from-yous, and one big congratulations. Then she came back into the room.

"Gordon? You have a breakfast date tomorrow?"

"Ohhh." I remembered.

Dad looked puzzled.

"Maureen," Ma said to him. "Tisdale-Morrissey."

Dad looked back at me. "The lady who just kicked your fanny all over the city? You want me to go with you, son?"

"Ha-ha, Dad. I can take her if she tries any rough stuff."

"Gord, I'm your father, and I'm not so sure."

The phone rang again. I whined to my mother. Then the FinsFone rang in my pocket.

"Shit. Dad?" I flipped him the phone and headed for the door. "Think you could handle that for me? Please?"

"Ah . . . what the hell," Dad said. "The old guy's had a tough year. I guess I could absorb a little gloat from him." He picked up. "Who? Who? I'm sorry, sir, but does Gordon know you? Are you a close personal friend?"

Dad was having himself a good time as I left.

She was sitting on her steps when I pulled up.

"Egads, a politician," Sweaty said. "I don't usually get into cars with known criminals."

I threw open her door. "Who you kidding, you do it all the time."

She hopped in, kissed and congratulated me. "I'm so proud," she said. "Champagne, Gordie. You know, it's the only thing for this."

I drove to the world's easiest liquor store. The place that sold me my first six-pack of Haffenreffer when I was fifteen using Mosi's fake ID that had his picture on it and that said I was twenty-seven years old. The place that had sold to me with six different IDs since that time.

"I can't sell to you, man," the clerk said.

"What are you talking about?" I rummaged

through my wallet for Fins's gold card, which I was sure would cinch it.

"Don't bother, man," he said. "Not only are you underage. Not only are you a celebrity right about now. But you are a celebrity mostly *because* you're underage. That would be pretty stupid, me selling to you with you all over the TV and everybody calling you 'The Kid.' "

He gestured over his shoulder at the little black-and-white TV, where the election was still the topic of the day. "No more screwing around for you, boy. You're a public figure."

With that, I turned and scuffed across the filthy floor to the exit.

"But I *will* give you a two-liter Sprite, free, if you give me your autograph."

I got back to the car, and I think my face told Betty the story. She was sympathetic, which was something, because when Sweaty Betty has a yen for champagne and doesn't get it . . .

"Scoot over," I said. "I'm exhausted. You want to drive for a while?"

"Do I want . . . ? Are you kidding?"

I shook my head, settled quietly into the passenger seat.

When I walked into the dining room of the Meridien, I felt special. Big-mucky-looking businesspeople all in the same suits were leaning hard into each other, making important points, at every table. A few of them even looked up at me as I was led to Maureen's spot at the far corner of the room. They grabbed quick looks, tossed me small nods of recognition, even made comments to each other as they gestured in my direction. It wasn't attention like, "Wow, there goes a big deal." It was more like, "Say now, there's something you don't see every day."

The polished-silver gleam of the place settings jumped up at me, as if they themselves were lighted rather than reflecting the chandeliers. There was a thickness to the room, carpeting that made you feel suspended off the floor, swirls of green-and-rust drapes hanging over the windows and falling all the way to the baseboards. I tried not to stare as I passed all the people who truly belonged here, but I couldn't help but be fascinated by the table manners that allowed them all to be intensely focused on each other, running the whole world, probably, while making the eating of a meal as neat and precise as Swiss watch repair.

It felt to me like the room was full of money and brains and style and the people who knew how it all worked.

I was wearing the same jacket and tie I had worn all the day before.

"Gordon, love, I could not be more proud of you."

She was more impressive in real life than she was on the radio or at the old softball games.

"Thank you, Mrs. Morrissey," I said, the first of the day's many sweats breaking out along my collar.

"Pshhh, *you* call me Maureen."

"But not Mo." I reminded her of Mad Matt.

"Correct."

We started eating, picking at the English muffins, cheese and apple Danish, toast, and black-currant jam the waiters kept bringing. The food was great, the service thing a treat, but I was uncomfortable.

"I told you you would come in fourth, didn't I?" she said brightly.

"You did. Thank you."

This, for some reason, made her laugh. "You're welcome. I had faith in you all along. You have a great many fine qualities, Gordie. You're a credit to your family."

I found myself floundering in a sea of strange, lightweight compliments and tangling myself in a net of awkward thank-yous.

"You ran a good race. Didn't embarrass yourself one bit."

"Thank you."

"Have every right to be proud. Your grandfather should be quite satisfied with all this."

"Thank you."

"Have some more juice, Gordie. Do let them bring you another eggs Benedict."

"Is that what that was?"

"You are refreshing," she said. "So, everything all right?"

"Can't think of anything I need."

"Tremendous." Maureen sat back in her chair, took a long sip of cranberry-orange juice, then lightly dabbed at the corners of her mouth with her stiff white napkin.

"The reason I invited you, Gordie, is that I like you. I think highly of you, and contrary to rumor, I like Fins very much too."

"Glad to hear that. So why'd you whip me so bad?"

She laughed. "Because that's the way it's going to be," she said, more seriously. "Gordie, enjoy your moment here. You finished fourth yesterday, and in the final, you're going to finish fourth again."

I didn't pick up right away. I thought she was playing the political angles to get an edge. "Oh, of course *you* say that. And at lunch you're probably going to tell the personal-injury billionaire that he's going to come in fourth. Then at dinner—"

"No, I'm not, Gordie. Because they're not coming in fourth, you are. And the only reason you're going to come in fourth is because there is no fifth place. Or sixth or seventh or seventy-seventh."

I put down my silverware, swallowed hard and dry on my last bite, and took it in.

"Wait a second here, wait a second," I said, throwing in a laugh mostly to calm myself and get back to the facts. "This is all going to be okay. See, I don't know if I'm supposed to tell you this, but it seems like the right time. Fins is gonna have a meeting with you. Really, I'm not even interested in the job. Fins just wanted . . . he's going to call you. You guys are going to have a talk, you're going to patch things up, and I'm going to step aside—gracefully."

"No," she said flatly. "No, we're not, and no, you're not. I have spoken with your grandfather, many times. But not for the purpose he thinks. Gordie, Fins is out, you see, and he's not getting back in. He just won't accept it. There will be no reconciliation. That exists in his head, and nowhere else."

There it swept me. I never wanted any part of this to start with, and I wanted it even less now, but I felt something there, something that hurt, and I wanted to beat it down. I saw, as Maureen's words landed on my head, I saw my da. I saw him as a little sad deluded person. I saw him as a towering figure brought down to the ground. I saw my da as a fool.

"You're wrong," I said, whether I believed it or not.

I stood up, making—for this place—a small scene. "You just want the fucking job, and you're afraid that me and my da are the only ones who can take it away from you."

Maureen stood across at the opposite side of the round table. Taller than me, slim, elegant but steely at the same time in her sleek gray suit, she quietly urged me to sit. When I wouldn't, she sat without me.

Then there was a hand on my shoulder. I looked up.

"Why don't you have a seat and let us explain," Saltonstall said.

I slipped back down into my seat under the weight of who he was. Saltonstall, the man with the real authority. The man who held the fund-raiser for me, and who had done it probably a hundred times for my grandfather over their many years as a team.

"What are you doing?" I asked him.

"I'm doing what I do," he said sincerely. "I know you're angry, son, but you've got to listen to this. Fins, he's been one of my best friends in the business. I will always love the man. But his time has passed."

"No it hasn't," I snapped.

Saltonstall nodded. "His time had passed *last* term, but he couldn't let it go. So we gave him one more. Out of respect. Then he changed his mind again, and we couldn't wait for him anymore."

"This is stupid," I said. "I won that spot in the final."

"A gift," he said calmly. "The fund-raiser? That was a testimonial to Fins. He truly is a beloved man in our circle. But the people there, they were there to salute and bon-voyage. None of them was voting for you in the final. It was a tribute to Fins. And the primary, that was a tribute to Fins, so he could go out a winner."

It started looking truer as I noticed that the prospective mayor, the woman who was such a force only minutes before, had shrunk completely in Saltonstall's shadow. They both looked so civil, here in this fine room, quietly doing what they were doing.

But he was my da. Whatever else he was—and I knew he was a lot of things—he was my da. He was always good to me and he was always big and grand and . . . and now he was like something felled, with all these jackals ripping pieces off of him while I watched.

"Fins just isn't dealing in the real world," she said, without meanness. "And he's trying to take you with him, Gordie. Why don't you just quit while you and your grandfather still look good, and it doesn't get embarrassing for everyone. Our people will help you devise a story that'll play well in the press."

I felt like a boxer who was not quite knocked out, but who couldn't answer the bell one more time either. I started to go.

"No, thank you," I said. "With all due respect, folks, you're not my team. I don't need to raise any more money, and I have my own campaign that's running just fine without you."

Saltonstall gestured way past me, to somebody across the room, as if he was summoning a waiter. I turned, and watched Bucky approach me, sadness and sorry smeared all across his fat rat face. I turned my back to him.

"But Da told me," I nearly pleaded. "He swears that his people still wanted him in. He's convinced."

"If we still wanted him in, Gordie . . ." Saltonstall said, and sighed. "If we still wanted him, he wouldn't be in jail."

"I'm afraid I've got some news you won't like. Before you say anything, I want you to hear me out. I love you, and I respect you, and nothing would make me happier than to make you happy, but as we both are men of the world, we both know things don't always work out. As sorry as I am to be bringing this up so soon after our big success in the primary, I think it's important to get it right out into the open: I'm afraid things are not going to work out quite the way you had hoped."

After three hours and a hundred and fifty practice speeches for my mirror, the words were working. I could do it.

Only, when the time came, I wasn't the one who spoke them. Da was.

"I know it isn't what you had planned, Gordie, but things have changed. She just ain't coming around, and so I figure, what the hell, right? Let's you and me make history. You could learn to love this, I swear it, the boy-mayor shtick. And now that I seen you in action, now that I seen ya crashing the party like you done, I know you can do it." Da turned to look over his shoulder. "Can't he, Chuckie? Can't the boy go all the way?"

Chuckie smiled and nodded, but it was different now. Even Chuckie the guard knew what Fins Foley didn't.

Fins didn't take the occasional puff of his oxygen tank anymore. He wore the mask strapped right onto his face, and towed the tank along behind him on wheels.

"And I'll be there, ta help ya, of course. All the way, boy, you know that."

All that practice didn't have me ready for this. I didn't have the guts for this, didn't have the heart, or the lungs, either. I could have used my own oxygen tank about then.

How do you do that? How do you pull the plug on somebody, when it all means so much?

"No, Da," I said softly.

"Well, sure, I knew you wasn't going to be crazy for the idea first off, but hang with me, Gordie. I promise you you're gonna love this in the end. You got great things comin' our way, a life you couldn't even a dreamed of."

"Da," I said, a little more emphatically. "No. No, I don't want the job, and I'm not going to want it tomorrow, and I'm never going to want it, and even if I did . . . *I don't have a goddamn chance of getting it.*"

Fins looked at me sideways. He looked back at Chuckie and gestured toward me with his thumb silently. Then, back to me. "You're just scared, that's completely—"

"Da!" I felt the whole building shrinking, squeezing on me, flipping, so that I felt like *I* was the prisoner, like *I* was never going to get out if I didn't move fast. "Da, don't you get it, you're out. Not temporarily, but permanently, all the way out."

He seemed to believe I was merely voicing an opinion.

"Na, not yet, Gordie. I ain't quite ready for that yet. I can't let it go."

"Nobody's asking you to let it go, Da. It's *gone*. All those great people you hooked me up with out there? They are the ones who told me. The primary? It was a gift, a retirement present for you. Your *people*, Da, that you keep telling me about, they did send you a message, but not the message you thought. The real message was Yes, we love you, old man, now get your ass out of the way."

My grandfather's already-cloudy gray eyes went softer as tears welled. With the steam fogging his acrylic oxygen mask, his famous face, his old bright beam, was nearly obscured.

But as he beat me to the words, I beat him to the crying.

I never wanted any of this. It started out as just so much stuff I didn't care about, and here I was coming apart over it.

After a long few minutes of watching each other

melt like a couple of late-March snowmen, he spoke to me.

"You have no right," my grandfather told me.

"I didn't do anything to you, Da." I didn't believe that.

"You have no right," he repeated, and it hurt more.

"I know I don't," I said. "But nobody else seems to be able to get the message across, so I think I need to try. Your time is over, Da. You've had your share. Your time was great. You got everything you wanted, and that has to be enough."

He stared at me coldly now, the glassiness gone, the stern, pondering face replacing it. As if he was considering my words, but I didn't think so.

"Well, Da, so what I've decided is, it's my time now. I'm a senior—have I mentioned to you that I'm a senior?—and I want to get what I can out of it while I can. The politics thing was your thing, it isn't mine. I just want my time, now. It's my time."

I was working hard to get something out of him, but it didn't seem to be paying. Finally a sly smile came over his wily old leather-face.

"It was Saltonstall, of course. I never could completely trust him, all these years. There was always that Yankee thing. . . . Anyway, it's too late for old Salty, because we got our money. This late in the game, we don't need no more. So we can cruise through to the final election, without . . ." He slapped his hands together hard and went right on strategizing, as if what

I'd told him was that a student volunteer, rather than the candidate, had left the campaign. He didn't slow down until Chuckie stopped him.

"Time, sir," Chuckie announced.

"Huh?" Fins asked.

"Time, gentlemen. Time's up. Visit's over. Kid," he said to me, firmly but not unkindly, "you have to leave now. Sir," he said to my da in a businesslike way, "time now."

Da smiled hard and gave me two high V-for-victory signs as he was led out, still talking strategy.

The next morning in homeroom we were sitting there half-conscious when Robert O'Dowd walked in.

First off, O'Dowd was not a member of this homeroom.

Second off, he was marching with a purpose, across the front of the class, ninety-degree left turn down the last aisle and all the way to the back, where Mosi and I were. Ignoring the laughter.

Third off, he had his underwear yanked all the way out of his pants, pulled up his back, over his head, with the remainder of the waistband hooked under his chin. A hall-of-fame wedgie.

"Wow" was all Mosi could say.

"Is it my birthday?" I asked.

O'Dowd clung to whatever dignity he could manage, speaking through his briefs.

"I was told I couldn't take it off until I came in here and you saw," he growled. "I was told to tell you you got nothin' to worry about from nobody. So now I told you." Then he left, tearing off the shreds of underwear as he ran.

What do you know, I thought. Fins *does* have goons. It's nice they let him keep his goons.

That was the day I finally remembered to go downtown and officially extricate myself from the nightmare that was the mayoral race. When I came out of the building, I felt like I was stepping out of the first good hot shower I'd taken in weeks.

I hadn't yet told Mad Matt I'd quit.

He was—on air—simultaneously congratulating me for making the mayoral final and relishing the inevitable drubbing I was going to absorb there. "As political exits go, Gordie, I'd say that at least beats getting shot in the head."

I had to laugh. It was the final relief, like being fired from a job you hate. I felt my position as talk-show clay pigeon being taken away as I was returned to the lowly technician-trainee job I'd wanted so badly.

"It does, Matt, it really does. And that's why I've quit the mayor's race. I figure nobody's going to shoot me here at the sound board."

"You did wha—?" Matt stopped himself. He did

not like getting caught being surprised on his own program. "Whoa! Cat's outta the bag now, huh? Guess everybody in the city's going to have to finally start believing in a Foley-free city now. Tell us, folks. Call and let us know *just* how devastated you are by the news." He cut to a commercial, swirled around in his chair, and glared at me. He made no attempt at further communication.

I couldn't really focus as I heard the beginning snickers when Sol fielded the fifth incoming phone call. When he transferred the call to Matt and the two of them then got happy, that was too much coincidence. I girded for the worst.

Which was exactly what I got.

"You don't have the guts to tell me yourself?" Fins said in a low, sickly, sad whisper. Not whisper enough, however, for any of us to escape the moment.

"I told you, Da," I said weakly. "I told you I couldn't go on, but you weren't listening to me."

"A legacy. A dynasty. I gave you everything I had accumulated, everything that was important to me. I passed it on to you. What you did? You spit on all that, then you go out, go on the radio, and you make a joke of me and everything I stand for."

There was a pause, the kind Matt always rushed to fill.

Nothing doing.

"You weren't a joke, Da. I didn't do that. Anyway, you told me you never listen to radio. Who told you—"

"You *owe* me," he said. "You didn't just quit on me, Gordie, you killed me."

He was being so totally unfair. I never wanted any of it. I told him that. He pushed it on me anyway. He lied to me. He tricked me. He was wrong, and he was totally unfair.

And I believed him.

"You killed me . . . and after all I . . . you, out of all the people . . . *you* killed me." He hung up.

I believe the show continued, but I have no recollection of it. I may have participated, may have not.

What I was well aware of was Mad Matt catching me on the way out the door.

"Sorry," I said, "about all that. About all everything. To tell you the truth, Matt, I'm going to be happy to get off the air, to just get in the background and learn the technician stuff like I came here for in the first place. I wasn't ever cut out for all that other stuff, you know?"

He shook his head slowly.

"No? No what?"

"What good could you possibly do me now? What did you think, Gordie, that I pulled your application out of a pile of a thousand other applications and all this stuff with your grandfather was just a *coincidence*? That was the shtick. Now the shtick is gone, and so are you."

I don't know why that should have hit me as a shock, but it did. I stood there with my tired jaw hanging open.

"I never even got to learn the technical stuff I came here to learn, because I was on the air all the time—which I never asked for."

He shrugged. "Showbiz is a cruel business, Gord. Good luck in your next endeavor. Whatever it is, I'm sure it will be eventful."

As he slammed the door behind him, I answered his nameplate.

"It sure *&@# won't be."

I woke in the morning to the sound of a couple of Fins's goons repossessing the car.

The Studebaker Gran Tourismo Hawk.

Which I loved more than anybody else did, even more than Fins did. Which I loved more than a person probably should love an inanimate object.

I heard the men downstairs making small talk with my dad. Dad small-talked back, not jolly, but not so strange that you couldn't tell he was pretty familiar with goondom—being Fins Foley's son. He didn't give them an argument, as I wouldn't have wanted him to. We all knew there were rules.

But that didn't make it hurt any less. One guy got into the royal-blue Continental they'd driven up in, while the other wedged his sloppy immensity into the driver's seat of a car that was not designed for his type. He chewed on a cigar as he eased the Tourismo backward down the driveway, and even though he didn't light up, he'd soiled it, spoiled it.

I watched out my upstairs window and nobody watched back, so it was okay. But I felt like I'd lost a lot as I lost that car. My car and my da's car.

But then, somebody *was* watching me. I don't know how he managed it, but as soon as the two cars had cleared the driveway, Mosi sprouted there in the middle of it, waving me to come on.

I dressed, went downstairs, and met my mother at the front door.

"What are *you* crying for?" I asked in a mock scold. I was trying not to get into the heaviness. She could melt me just like that, and I had to head it off. I couldn't be melted now, not with the smell of the Studebaker still in the driveway.

"I'm sorry," she sniffed. "I mean, certainly I'm glad you are out of that insane political thing—"

"And the insane radio thing."

"Yes. But as I said in the beginning, I don't necessarily support all your ideas, but I support you, Gordie."

She was doing it. I was getting squishy.

"Maaaa. I have to go to school. Please . . ."

"Okay. Anyway, I think it all stinks. I can't stand to see anything taken from you. That car was yours."

I smiled. I mean, she hadn't actually given me anything—I was still walking—but then she had, hadn't she?

I went out and started down the driveway, and she stopped me. *Pssst.*

"I'm not supposed to tell you, but I don't see why I shouldn't: Your father did vote for you. He couldn't resist."

The telling of that seemed to make her feel so good. The hearing of it made me feel so good.

I met Mosi at the foot of the drive. I'd forgotten how much I liked walking.

"A BEATING OF BIBLICAL PROPORTIONS," trumpeted *The School Newspaper*. I was not, apparently, going to be student body president either.

The candidates are required—kind of a throwback to sitting in the stocks on the town common—to go around and take down all of their old posters the day after the beating. Mosi, ever the sport, helped me.

"So, you all sad and stuff now?" he asked as he stripped off the few remaining strands of a poster in the gym.

"Um . . ." I felt it out as I spoke. "Yes, I suppose so. Not the *what*, really, since none of that crap was what I wanted anyhow, but more the *how*. The how hurt. 'Cause I got sucked in, to the whole glam thing, and wound up wanting what I didn't really even want, then getting all twisted up and slapped around and then left with nothing to show at all."

"Hmmm," Mosi said. "I think I follow. Can I say something?"

I shrugged. And meant it.

"I'm kinda not too sad you lost."

"You don't say."

"Promise you won't get mad."

"I promise."

"I kinda . . . didn't help you."

"So what, Mos? In the end, I kinda didn't help myself."

By this time we had gathered most of the Foley campaign debris and were out on the football field, heading for the poster on the end-zone wall.

"No, Gordie, I mean, I *really* didn't help. Like, *a lot* I didn't help."

"Spit, Mosi."

"I was in the I-Team."

There was a long silence between us. When I turned on him, he was raising his hands in self-defense.

"Duh, Mosi. I mean, how could I *not* know it was you?"

"Oh, ya," he said. "You're so smart, tell me why I did it, then. 'Cause *I* don't even know why I did it, so howdya like that?"

"Yes you do. We've been talking about this senior thing for three years now, what all we were going to do and how fun it would be. Then we got there, we weren't having any of it, because of all the stupid shit I was doing. I didn't have the brains to quit, so you did it to me, like one of those mercy killings old couples do to each other."

As I said it, I remembered the reason Mosi was always my friend, often my only close friend. The thing that tended to make Mosi different from everybody else, as if he wasn't already different from everybody else. Mosi cared.

"Thanks," I said. "Ya friggin' dope."

"You're welcome," he said, smiled, and slapped me a little too hard.

"You know, Mos," I said, rubbing my cheek. "You were the only person other than my grandfather—and *he's* demented—to actually think I had a chance to win."

He sat on the ground near me. "I was pretty worried for a while there," he said seriously.

In bed that night I lay there trying to pull it together. What happened?

I killed my da—that's what he said. But I rediscovered my Mosi. I found out stuff about myself by finding out what I was not. I was not Fins Foley's boy, which was good. But I was not his grandson anymore either.

I found out that the price, for finding out, is high.

I was not political timber, and I was not a media star.

The rest was still out there, to be found out.

I turned on the radio, tuned in to Matt's show and my new replacement intern/personality. The nature of the talk had clearly shifted away from politics. Tonight's subject was titled "The Seven Deadly Erogenous Zones."

"And we have a challenge," Matt wheezed. "Sweaty Betty urges our listeners, male and female, to call in and name them all."

"Or to ask advice on all things worldly," Betty kicked in.

Now this, I thought, was a show. *This* made sense. Here was a bona fide media personality, and a person who knew who she was.

I smiled, pulled out the FinsFone, which had not yet been canceled, and I dialed.